IMPRACTICAL MAGIC

VIVIENNE SAVAGE

CHAPTER 1

River Jackson jerked awake from a nap to the drone of a lawnmower through the living room window. The glorious Texas sunlight slanted across her face, but her chest still heaved with panicked breaths from the dream of a malignant force spreading over her town. In that nightmare, swarms of locusts had blotted out the sun like bleak clouds.

I was asleep. Only sleeping, she told herself.

Groaning, River sat up and ran her fingers through her disheveled brown curls. She'd stayed up late studying her spellbook and attempting scrying spells to investigate the magical force creeping into the San Antonio area. While it wasn't her job to police the darkness, the enigmatic Mystic Trinity governing all witches had demanded everyone to pitch in.

Clearly, she'd listened to their doom and gloom too long, and it had finally seeped into her brain.

As she shook off the nightmare's grip, she became aware of the sexy neighbor pushing his mower outside. She parted the blinds to scope out a better look and sighed in appreciation.

Zacarias, the hottie next door, had the build of an MMA fighter. Tattoos sprawled over his bronzed skin and defined muscles, but most of them covered his gorgeous back. While he could hire out a landscaper, he always did the work himself, resembling a half-dressed Latin American god deserving his own temple.

Contrary to her ogling, the best part of having an amazing neighbor wasn't his athletic physique—it was the generosity prompting Zac to mow *her* half of the property too. It all started one morning when he came out and caught her tidying his sad and lonely little flower bed in the front yard. In return, he cut her grass that evening. Shirtless. Glistening, with all of his muscles exposed from the carved V at his hips to his spectacular chest.

A full sleeve of rainforest-themed tattoos covered his left arm, a colorful mural depicting the Amazon. The tropical birds, prowling jaguars, and verdant splendor made River ache to find an excuse to examine them up close. With her fingers. Maybe with her mouth too.

Damn, girl, it hasn't been that long. Single and free of any relationship, she'd been living the life of a girl on her own for a few months since a less-than-amicable breakup between her and a firefighter from Austin.

Stretching again and letting her joints pop, she shrugged off the lingering exhaustion then shambled into the kitchen to her automated tea maker.

A few minutes passed before the brewing cycle completed. The invigorating scent of ginger and lemongrass wafted up to her as she poured the electric kettle's contents into a non-glass pitcher. Because she'd learned the hard way what happens when glass goes from hot to cold in three seconds flat.

River wore four different rings and multiple wrist bangles as part of her everyday wardrobe, each item of jewelry a vital piece of equipment used to channel magic. Some had been crafted by her mother with love, others made by River alongside her mentor. And since she'd left the frost band in the freezer overnight a week ago, it held a complete charge for ice magic.

Skating her finger over the edge of the pitcher instantaneously reduced the steaming liquid to near freezing. She added sprigs of mint and stevia then wandered away to tidy her hair. Hopefully she could do something that didn't involve hacking it all off with a pair of scissors in frustration.

Ugh. Maybe she would go to the salon after all, a quick visit to break free from the cycle of untamable ponytails and lazy updos. While she lacked the time or inclination for extreme makeovers, she needed relief from the stress of managing her wild mane of coils and dark spirals.

"Do I want to impress the hot neighbor?" She examined her reflection in the bathroom mirror, pursed her lips thoughtfully, then tugged the entire mess into a satin scrunched band. Nope. Not worth the effort.

Besides, he was probably already taken.

Balmy air greeted her when she stepped into the grass-scented outdoors. Ice cubes clinked together within the two tall glasses in her hands as she navigated the cement path and walked toward Zac. He'd stopped to mop his brow with a handkerchief.

"Hey!" River called.

Startled, he whipped around, his green eyes growing wide with surprise. "You were home?"

"Uh-huh."

He glanced at her empty drive.

"My car's in the garage for once. I had it detailed yesterday." She beamed. "Maybe you should do the same."

"That's next on the agenda." His big grin dimpled his left cheek. She melted and stared longer than intended.

"Anyway, I figured since you're always doing this ninja-lawnmowing thing into my yard, the least I could do was bring you a cold drink." While biting her lower lip, she dragged one toe over the grass-strewn cement path. "I could help you with your car too. It's a nice day."

A fine layer of dust and pollen dulled the metallic black paint job on Zac's Jaguar, turning it green. He twisted around to look at his vehicle and frowned. "Yeah, maybe I should since it looks like there was a tree orgy beside it."

"Yeah, well, now you know to keep it in the garage since we have so many trees around here." She passed over his glass then knelt beside her herb garden. A tidy row of river stones displayed the names of each plant, their species painted on each flat rock. Basil, mint, and rosemary grew alongside less common herbs like lavender and mugwort. The larger garden sprawled across her portion of their backyard.

"Why do you grow so much sage and stuff anyway?"

"Some people cook with it, you know." The last time she brought up the truth about her Pagan practices in

Texas, she had received raised brows and some lecturing about the Devil's handiwork.

Zac gave her a doubtful look. "That's a lot of cooking."

"I use it for sage bundles too. Homemade incense. Soaps. Sachet bags. Stuff like that. When I have a good harvest, I sometimes sell the extra at the farmers' market."

"Aren't sage bundles and all that herb-burning stuff used by priests and hippies?"

His perplexed expression made her giggle. "They're used in lots of cultures and religions. Smudging was a ritualistic ceremony used by many Native American peoples, but today most modern day pagans and witches use smoke cleansing rituals as a way of banishing negative energy."

"Fair enough." He chugged down his tea. "Let me set this down. Then we can start on my car. If you were serious, I mean."

"Well, you did help me get my computer back online after I screwed it up. I think I can handle a little car wash."

"Great. I'll be right back then." Zacarias set his empty glass on her porch.

When he jogged away to his garage, River took advantage of the view and watched the tight rear under his low-riding gym shorts. The taut muscles in his back shifted beneath colorful ink and made him into a living work of art.

He returned with a bucket, sponges, soap, and the garden hose. After he had rinsed the pollen and leaves from the car's surface, they divided the task of scrubbing it together.

"Looking a little soapy there, River."

"Huh?" A few suds covered her hands and clung to her arms. She glanced up and saw Zac pointing the bright yellow hose nozzle in her direction. "Don't you dare! I mean it, Zac—"

The merciless spray pelted her, a shock of cold water on her upper chest and face. She shrieked and ran to the other side of the car, where she ducked and used the vehicle as a shield.

"Asshole!" She flung the sponge at him in retaliation.

"Hahaha. I'm done, I'm done. Promise."

River remained behind the car, half-crouched to conceal her body from his eyes. The T-shirt and cotton bralette plastered against her skin provided insufficient cover. She shivered and shot him a dirty look.

Not that I have much to hide, or he'll even care, she thought.

Suppressing her modesty, River straightened and glowered at him.

"I'll finish up. You head inside and get dry," Zac suggested.

"Gee, I wonder who I have to thank for that."

His grin widened. "You looked hot, so I cooled you off a little. You're *very* welcome for the aid. Now scoot."

Even after she went inside, Zac remained on her mind. His carefree laughter and warm smiles, the way his eyes twinkled vivid-green in the sunlight. She sighed, smitten and infatuated.

After tossing her sopping wet clothes in the washer, she yanked a clean top from the dryer and tugged it on without another bra.

Her blonde and slim, model-perfect mother never failed to point out ways to improve her bottom-heavy figure. While River had her mom's modest boobs, she hadn't inherited her metabolism. From her dad, she'd received the genes to easily pack on muscle if she hit the gym. Even now, years after retiring from the NFL, her athletic father still outperformed men half his age.

Her mom used to tease that she was a changeling, swapped at birth by fairies, because River's facial features bore no close resemblance to *either* of them and could have been any couple's biracial child.

Once she squeezed into another pair of yoga pants, she rolled the top down beneath her rounded tummy, made a promise to do more sit-ups, and slid onto the chair in front of the computer desk.

A new e-mail waited for her from a repeat client.

Zacarias didn't know it, but he served as inspiration for some of the book covers River designed. The bronze shade of his skin, the tattoo quality, and even the way he moved had invaded her digital masterpieces with a subtle touch.

Work didn't provide the necessary distraction she'd needed from Zac's pecs, and after an unsuccessful hour of painting tattoos on some model's torso in Photoshop, she resorted to meditation and yoga.

A few minutes after turning on the essential oil diffuser, the sweet, rich scent of sandalwood pervaded the room. She sat on a silk rug reserved for her quiet introspections, closed her eyes, and breathed in a deep, rhythmic pattern.

A knock interrupted her five minutes in.

"Honestly," she muttered as she rose. "Can't I get *anything* done today?"

The knocker banged again.

"I'm coming!"

Zac's hulking shadow loomed outside, visible through the stained glass. He flashed a charming grin once she opened the door. "In the mood for a peace offering?"

He wore dark jeans and a black muscle shirt revealing his broad shoulders and inked biceps. It took her a moment to realize he'd come with gifts, her gaze lowering to the large serving platter in his hands. Steak, portobello mushrooms, and purple asparagus covered it from edge to edge. The smell, tangy and earthy, was absolutely divine. Her stomach gurgled in anticipation.

"Do you always make enough for two?"

Had one of his sexy dates stood him up, allowing her to reap the benefits? Did any of the women she expected him to date even eat steak?

She chastised herself in silence. Assuming all thin girls subsisted on air was as cruel and inaccurate as thin girls assuming she lived on cheesecakes and patty melts all day.

Okay, so she did. Sometimes. Lately, she'd tried to step up her dieting game by including more vegetables and less chocolate, but it hadn't done much for changing her figure. But she did feel good, and that mattered more than shrinking a few inches from her waistline.

"You brought me tea and helped with my car. The least I can do is feed you in return. So… may I come in?"

"A bottle of wine might have upped your chances, but since you went through all the work…"

"Look under the tray."

He'd cradled a bottle of red wine between his arms and the tray.

With a sweep of her hand, she welcomed him inside. She'd have to be a crazy person to turn down a free meal and bottle of wine with a sweetheart like Zacarias. "If you put that on the table, I'll grab some plates, glasses, and silverware."

As two halves of a duplex, their homes were mirror opposites with two bedrooms and a bath on the upper level, a living room, small bedroom, kitchen, dining room, half-bath, and a breakfast nook on the ground floor. Her television hung above the fireplace opposite the desk housing the computer. A sofa bordered one wall, although it was more like two joined recliners than a loveseat.

River glanced at her guest to see his attention fixed on the computer screen. She'd been in the process of painting black tribal tattoos on a naked male torso. A huge jaguar roared in the background some brawny model's sculpted abdomen and hairless pecs.

"Uh…" Heat rushed to her cheeks. Times like this made her grateful that her darker complexion masked her blushes.

"Book covers, right?"

She ducked her head in a quick nod. "Yeah. Helps pay the bills, between that and my other work."

"I got curious after I fixed your computer and checked out your portfolio," he confessed. "Your work is great. Really. If you didn't already have an awesome business of your own, I'd try to steal you to work as an illustrator at my company."

"Well, if you ever need a freelancer, keep me in mind. You know, like promo stuff or something. I do concept art when I have the time."

Zac owned his own business and had recently merged with another company less than a year ago. The deal had made him filthy stinking rich, from what she'd read in the paper, yet he'd chosen to move to her modest neighborhood in Atropos, Texas. Although it was less than a half hour from San Antonio, their rural town couldn't be found on the map.

River disappeared into the kitchen and returned with utensils. Zac hovered near her computer, presumably admiring her work. He peered at the author name. "So, I was hanging around social media and heard some crap claiming Sassy Sizzle isn't really a woman. Any truth to that?"

"What makes you think I know?" she countered, setting the plates on the coffee table.

"You've done all of her covers ever since she went self-pub. Figured you were close."

She twirled a curl around her finger, stretching the spiral and letting it snap back a few times before releasing it. Sassy Sizzle, her favorite author, was a gay Latino guy from Dallas, Texas. She knew because they'd met for the first time a year ago for coffee, dinner, and a musical.

Zac would have to torture her to get the truth from her lips.

"We are close, and really, even if she was a man, why should it matter? The books are sexy."

For lack of a dining room table, they settled on her couch instead. She passed Zacarias a plate then made her own, taking modest portions.

"Damn straight they are. I was just going to ask if you knew when the next one would hit the stores."

River blinked. "I didn't take you for the type to read romance novels," she said while cutting the first bite. She raised it to her mouth, and then the flavors exploded against her tongue, making her both envious of his cooking skills and angry she'd probably stuff her face in front of him.

He shrugged nonchalantly. "I'm not really. Like I said, after we talked, I looked up some of your work on your website, followed some links, and I ended up reading a little."

"How'd you find my site?"

"I'm a computer geek. I know how to google," he replied, rolling his eyes.

Yeah, a freaking hot computer geek who breaks every stereotype ever uttered about video game designers and computer programmers. She sighed.

"That's a hot photo you have up on your site, by the way."

His comment caught her unprepared. Luckily, she had already swallowed her mouthful of steak, staving off a disaster. She stared at him through large eyes, half expecting him to follow it up with a joke.

"Hot? Me?"

"It's a really good shot of you. I've never seen you in a dress before."

As a rule, she never wore dresses that didn't fall below her knees, not wanting to show her chunky thighs. A close friend, who happened to be a photographer, promised he'd take the pictures from slimming angles and work all kinds of magic without using Photoshop.

"I actually borrowed that dress from a friend."

"Shame."

Clearing her throat, River shifted away to a more harmless, neutral topic. "So, uh, while I have you here, I was thinking about expanding the front garden. Is it cool if I use your yard too?"

He shrugged. "Fine with me. I'm hopeless with flowers. I either kill them with too much water or not enough."

"Maybe you should stick with a rock and succulent garden," she teased.

"Smartass."

River grinned.

Over conversation, they finished most of dinner and drained the entire bottle of wine together before Zac ambled to the door. He'd offered to help wash dishes, but she waved him off and walked him to the stoop.

Standing barefooted, she came up to his shoulder, and lingering beside him by the doorway made her wonder if she should throw caution to the wind and lean in for a hug. Or a kiss. A pleasant buzz courtesy of the wine filled her with wicked ideas.

Zacarias interrupted her thoughts. "Hey. Do you have a black cat?"

She blinked up at him. "No, why do you ask?"

"Oh." Disappointment flit over his handsome features. He frowned. "There was a black cat I was thinking of taking in. I haven't seen her around lately, but I used to spot her near your balcony sometimes."

"I've seen her around. She plays in the woods behind our place." It wasn't a direct fib, at least.

Giving in to her more innocent impulses, she hugged Zac, thanked him for dinner, and then watched him jog across the yard. Afterward, she rushed upstairs to her bedroom and cracked open the balcony door.

River's fingers wrapped around the cat's eye pendant dangling from her neck. It became warm and alive in her hand, polished smooth with a perfect oval shape. A vertical line of green divided it down the middle and reminded her of Zac's eyes.

"Well, now. I can't let him worry about me."

***

Zac's catchy R&B ringtone reached him from the kitchen counter when he stepped into the house. A glance at the caller ID revealed his ex-wife's phone number and a few missed calls.

Disgruntled, he weighed the options and decided declining the call would only give her an excuse to visit in person. Then she'd be at his door in her overpriced Louboutins pleading for him to let her in.

"Shit." Zac jabbed his finger into the green button and raised the phone to his ear. "We've talked about this. I don't want to see or talk to you."

"But I'm only five minutes away, sweetie," Lucia cooed over the line. "Trust me, you'll be glad to see me this time."

The last time he'd met Lucia had been in court on the day of their divorce, three months after discovering she'd slept with her agent *and* her photographer. And everybody else who was willing to dive between her legs.

It didn't matter to him that the relationship had gone downhill months earlier because he couldn't trust her to be honest about when the affairs began.

Fuming, he thought of the first signs of her infidelity— when the sex dried up and she became defensive about her cell phone. They had made love for the last time a month before Zac discovered the truth, engaging in lackluster and passionless sex after he'd taken her out for a night on the town to her favorite places.

All night long, Lucia had behaved like she was obligated to be there on his arm. He'd taken her out for dinner and dancing, but she sulked and checked out her text messages.

Almost two years had passed since their divorce, and he had no desire to try again. Lucia, apparently, was having second thoughts. She'd been hounding him for a reconciliation since the summer began after a year of silence.

"Well turn around and head back to the city."

"Don't be ridiculous. I'm already on your road, so I'll see you in a few minutes." Lucia disconnected the call.

Zac clenched his jaw and growled.

Meoowww.

A black feline stood on her hind legs at the back door, pawing and mewling gently for attention. She used to visit weekly until her recent disappearance, making Zacarias wonder if her owner lived in the area. He let her in. With her tail raised high, she prowled past him then twined between his ankles.

"Well, look who finally showed back up."

Meow.

"You may not wanna stick around today," he muttered to the cat. "My ex is dropping by, and she can be a real bitch."

The feline jumped up and scaled his jeans until Zac pulled her into his arms. Her head was soft as velvet, warm when she rubbed against his cheek. He closed his eyes and sighed.

"Do you have an owner? Or do you live alone out there somewhere, without a home?"

She purred and pressed one of her paws against his chin.

"I missed you too, *gatinha.*"

Zacarias opened a can of tuna onto a dish and set it on the floor. She hurried to it with her tail raised high, and then she softly mewled as if giving her appreciation. He smiled. "*De nada.* You're always welcome here, you know." He didn't think she understood, but it was nice to chat with another creature who lacked expectations or ulterior motives. River was the only person in the neighborhood, besides the nameless kitty, who didn't see him as a walking stack of bills.

Minutes later, Lucia pulled into the drive behind his Jag. He met her at the door.

"Surprise," she chirped, holding a bottle of pink champagne in one hand and a Manila folder in the other.

He sighed. "What are you doing here, Lucia?" As his gaze swept over her slim physique from top to bottom, he tried to remember what once attracted him. The plastic woman on his porch wasn't Luce; she was a simulacrum crafted by her agent and the modeling world. Red-dyed hair trailed over her shoulders like flames, she'd lost another twenty pounds, and she'd had work done on her nose along with injections to her lips.

She ignored his unenthusiastic welcome. "I found a buyer for the house."

His brows shot up. "Really?"

"Really," Lucia said with a pleased smile on her face. "I decided not to stall it out anymore. Their offer is about forty grand less than what you wanted, but—"

"I'll take it. Let's just get it out of our hands."

After welcoming her inside, Zac led the way to the kitchen table where she spread the paperwork and set down the bottle of bubbly wine.

He hated pink champagne but would humor her to be polite. To be the bigger person and show he wasn't bitter.

While she retrieved a pair of glasses from the cabinet, he broke the seal and popped the cork, ignoring her coy smile.

"Sorry, but… I forgot to bring a pen," she said. "Do you have one on hand?"

"Just a sec," Zacarias replied. When he returned with a pen from the personal office upstairs, he found Lucia and the cat in a staring contest. The cat's back was arched. She hissed and spat at his ex-wife, behaving with hostility he'd never witnessed in her before.

"Where did you get this animal?" Lucia demanded. "It tried to attack me!"

"What? What did you *do* to make her attack you?" he countered.

Her eyes grew wide. "I didn't do anything but pour our drinks!"

He glanced at the feline, uncertain. "All right. All right. Maybe you moved too quickly and scared her." He sat opposite his ex and read the paperwork. It looked legitimate; the offer was lower than his asking price, but he'd accept the loss to remove the final link between them.

"What do you think about it?" Lucia asked.

"I think $365,000 isn't awful."

The cat leaped into his lap and sniffed the glass, practically putting her face into it. "Hey, whoa. That's not good for you." He plucked it out of her reach and sipped. It tasted rank, a funny aftertaste clinging to his tongue afterward.

The bottle he'd shared with River was better.

"So get to the point," he muttered. "What do you want from me, and why are you buttering me up with champagne? You knew I'd accept this offer. You didn't need to bribe me."

The cat knocked the glass off the table. Zac saw it happening and knew what to expect, but his reflexes couldn't compete with an impetuous little furball. Glass flew in every direction, skittering shards across the floor around a puddle of pink bubbly.

"Shit."

"That little bitch!"

Pink spots stood out against Lucia's pristine white dress, but most of the puddle was on the floor. He bit back the urge to laugh. "Calm down. She's a cat, and it was an accident." *A cat who deserves another plate full of tuna fish after this.*

Her gray eyes narrowed. "It figures you'd take a cat's side over mine. I guess it shouldn't surprise me, considering your little secret."

Always the drama queen. He sighed. "Look, I'm glad the house is selling, but you could have said as much over the phone. Have the lawyers fax me anything else related to the sale that I don't need to sign in person."

"Can you blame me for wanting to see you again? I *miss* you."

Did you miss me when you had David's dick in your mouth? he wondered. "Uh-huh."

After scooping up the cat, he took her to the door and let her outside, wishing it was as easy to make Lucia leave.

Wasn't it as easy? It was his damned house, and the longer he considered the consequences of scooping his ex into his arms and depositing her on the lawn, the more appealing the idea became.

"Why do you let strays in anyway?" she complained.

"My house," he gritted at her. He took the first step, intending to act through on his urge to hurl her from the property with the intensity of a discus thrower.

"I've been a rude guest," she said in a sudden change of tone. She hurried on her stiletto heels to the counter where she tugged a few sheets from the paper towel roll. "Let me clean up this mess, and then I'll get out of your hair." She smiled politely, but it was thin, brittle, and as phony as their marriage.

"I've got it."

"But—" She stopped and snapped her painted lips shut. After a moment, she offered the wadded-up paper towels. "As you like, Zacarias. I'll see myself out."

"That's probably for the best."

Lucia collected the form and flashed him a smile. "Sorry to interrupt your evening. I'll let you know when everything proceeds." She kissed his cheek, no doubt leaving a smear of red lipstick behind, then strode out the door. He exhaled a sigh of relief that it was over.

No matter how much he missed the relationship they'd once had, he would never become desperate enough to let her back into his life again.

Those days were over.

CHAPTER 2

River popped out of her feline shape and onto two legs again. After the disorienting sensation wore off, she hurried downstairs and peeked out the window at Zac's half of the duplex.

"She's a freaking witch!" she exclaimed to the empty room. "Zac was married to a witch. Does he even know?"

The bigger question was, now that she knew her neighbor had been married to a witch, what the hell did she do with what she'd just learned?

The moment Zac left the room for a pen, Lucia had brought a small vial from her purse and poured its contents into his glass. River couldn't let him drink it, even without knowing the purpose of the mystery drug.

In feline form, she had a heightened sense of smell and a cat's reflexes. Hints of catnip and damiana had wafted to her from the bubbly drink. Instinct had taken over the moment she had her chance.

"Worse than roofies," River muttered. It had to be a lust potion, as damiana was a common ingredient used in sex magic.

Or hangovers, she chided herself. A funny feeling in her tummy told her not to give the other witch the benefit of the doubt.

Some witches didn't view love potions as dark magic, believing them to be innocent and innocuous enchantments. Their governing council, the Daughters of the Moon, even saw them in shades of gray. River's beliefs differed. In the wrong hands, they robbed an individual of control over their body and actions. A loyal husband would cheat on his wife of twenty years. A new bride could sleep with another man.

In her eyes, it was no better than date rape or sexual assault, and most witches agreed with her. Lust spells were for adding a little kink to a relationship or helping a willing lover out of a poor mood—not for reeling in exes who had moved on.

"I can't even tell him. I mean, how do I tell a guy, 'oh, by the way, your ex-wife tried to spike your celebration bubbly with a rip-off of love potion number nine' when I wasn't even supposed to be in the room? Ugh."

She had to give his ex some credit for being a good sweet talker. They chatted outside by her sporty, flamboyant red Mustang. The color matched her shitty dye job.

"Don't fall for her tricks, Zac. Send her packing," River grumbled while spying through the blinds.

The wait was excruciating. Each second ticked by at the pace of molasses. Finally, after what seemed like hours—but was only minutes—Lucia slid behind the wheel.

After her sporty coupe vanished around the corner, River returned upstairs and dropped to her knees beside the bed. The heavy trunk beneath it contained all her spellworking supplies, including an old Book of Ways passed down through her family from her great-great-grandmother. Each generation, the witch before River had added her favorite spells and potion recipes to the book, including her own mother. One day, River would add to it and pass the hefty heirloom to her daughter.

She breathed in the musty, old book smell and traced her fingers over the leather cover. She could have sold the book for a mint on the paranormal market, but nothing would ever part it from her possession.

Sitting cross-legged on the floor, she opened the first book and searched through the pages, murmuring under her breath, "Love spells, love spells."

Although alchemy hadn't always been River's strong suit, the more she dabbled in it, the more she improved in unmistakable leaps and bounds. It would be easier if she knew exactly what Lucia had used. Brewing resembled cooking in some ways—substituting a single ingredient could lead to the same result with a wholly different flavor. Or maybe give a guy a hard-on able to endure most of the night instead of lasting only one romp. Or make him fuck like a beast, instead of making love like a gentleman. If only she'd stolen a sample of it to know what Lucia had intended for Zacarias.

River studied every line about lust spells, sex magic, and enchantments affecting the heart until, in a moment of hair-tugging frustration, she pushed the book aside.

Witches shouldn't have had so many ways to lead a man around by the balls.

"Right then, I'll have to go see Pythia soon," she mused.

She didn't speak with Zacarias again, but she did spot him in the backyard, presumably searching for the black cat. Guilt darted a lance into her chest when she considered her deceitful behavior. Maybe his ex was a bitch for attempting to spike his drink, but what made her dishonesty any better?

Then again, pretending to be a lovable kitten and pouring a drug into a man's drink were leagues apart.

It seemed innocent months ago when she'd first wandered past him and discovered his affection for kitties. At first, he'd watched her traipse across the yard, but she'd delayed entering the house for fear of him connecting the dots and later asking if she owned a pet.

Then he'd approached and checked her for a collar, even taking River to his kitchen and feeding her leftover steak. Every damned bite had been delicious, and worth being his captive for an afternoon while he chatted about his game business. Zacarias had held her on his lap for a movie, kissed her whiskered face, and mused out loud, wondering if he'd kidnapped someone's pet.

He'd even picked up the phone and called the local police station to ask if anyone had reported a missing animal. She escaped later that evening by lingering near the door and crying until he let her go.

Every so often, she ventured out in her feline shape and poked her nose, literally, into his life. She did the things she could never do as a human, too shy to grab him by his face and sweetly kiss him.

And now, he wanted to adopt her into his home as an actual pet. She sighed and swallowed back the guilt, deciding to focus on the more immediate issue on hand—Lucia's evil plot.

Whatever action she took against Lucia for breaking the unspoken code of ethics governing their kind, it was too important to make a spur of the moment decision. She needed to consult with a more knowledgeable witch, and in the meantime, protect Zac from another immoral seduction.

***

The next day brought a second chance to spend time with Zac. He visited at half past noon, holding a recent houseplant purchase. It was a sad little thorny plant with vibrant red-pink flowers in a white ornamental pot.

"My begonia is dying, and I'm not sure why."

"This is a bougainvillea. Not a begonia," she corrected him. "They mislabeled it at the greenhouse. I think it'll grow better outside too. Maybe we can plant it in your garden?"

He frowned. "Well, shit. I wanted something to add some color to the *inside* of my place."

"How about I give you one of my orchids?" River offered. "I collect so many, I'm sort of tired of caring for them all." She passed the bougainvillea back then waved for Zac to follow her into the living room. Once she'd scooted into the desk chair, her fingers flew over the keys. Heat rushed to her face when she realized she'd left open the site to one of her favorite herbal suppliers while researching the possible ingredients of Lucia's lust potion. A list of aphrodisiac components filled the screen with suggestive uses.

"So, you're into that herbal remedy and supplement stuff, huh?" Zac asked from behind her.

"Um, yup."

"My ex was too. She'd order the most expensive tiny bottles of crap," he said with a laugh. "Never explained much about it to me. Said she was into essential oils. So do they work?"

River bit her lower lip. Most witches were secretive about their true talents. The world was long past hanging, drowning, and burning people at the stake, but magic was as much a closely guarded secret as the shapeshifters she sometimes crossed.

Nothing about Zac's behavior implied he knew anything about the paranormal world.

She sighed. "As far as I can see, it works. I have trouble… anxiety problems. You should have seen me in college. Sometimes I think I only managed to get through it all with the help of a few drops of passionflower and lavender each night."

"Huh. Well, maybe one day you can recommend something for concentration that won't make me sneeze for hours."

"You have a sensitive nose?" she asked, tilting her face up to him and grinning. "Are you one of those people who can't tolerate chemicals?" With Zac standing behind the desk chair, leaning against it with one arm propped on the back of it, he was close enough for her to pick up the subtle smell of ordinary soap against his skin.

"Yeah, you could say that. Most perfumes and stuff make my nose itch. Can't stand 'em."

After moistening her lips with her tongue, she concentrated on the computer screen again and brought up some landscaping examples. "These are bougainvillea like yours. See how lovely they look outside?"

"That is nice," he agreed. "Can you do something like that?"

"I think so. Come spring. It's a little late in the season to plant it outdoors now. So… for now, you'll have to keep it inside for a while longer. I'm gonna guess you kept it on your computer desk, where you type away all of the night like a vampire video game programmer."

"Guilty as charged."

She chuckled. "Well, until we can plant this outside, you'll need to put it somewhere closer to a window. These plants need more light than your desk lamp can provide." She tilted her head slightly to the side, considering him for a moment before continuing. "So, why'd you pick this one?"

"My mother grows plants like these where she and my stepfather live," he replied. "I never asked why she keeps them outdoors." His bashful smile endeared River to him even more.

"Where does your mother live? Further south?"

Zacarias laughed. "You could say that. She moved from Texas back to Brazil when my father died a couple years ago. Then she met her current husband and decided to do the whole marriage thing again."

"I'm sorry to hear that."

"Sorry my dad died, or sorry she remarried?"

The quip caught her by surprise. She stared at his reflection in the computer screen, resembling a deer in the headlights.

Zac idly toyed with one of River's curls—if he wasn't so hot, she would have had serious words—stretching the coil and letting it spring back into place. "Chill, Riv. It's okay. I like him. He's a nice guy, and he makes her happy. It's strange to see her married to someone else, but he treats her well, and that's all that matters."

She exhaled a deep breath of relief. "You're a good son."

"I am," he agreed, flashing an infectious grin.

"Anyway, come upstairs with me real quick. I wanna show you something."

Upstairs, she took him past the meditation room and into the master bedroom where she'd left a fresh load of panties and bras spread over the Nightmare Before Christmas themed duvet.

Dammit. Heat spread down the back of her neck and across her shoulders when Zac's eyes drifted over the bed. The scattered pairs of undies were boring shades: white, pink, some striped and dotted. Fortunately, none were granny panties.

"You have a lot of orchids," Zac commented. His eyes then roved over a photo of River and her dad in a small 5 x 7 frame. Her mother had taken the picture after a skating competition when River was seventeen. She'd won.

"I told you, I collect them."

Tidy rows of white shelves lined the wall beside the balcony, each one crowded with her favorite knick-knacks and books. Small pots of miniature orchids added pops of color amidst worn, dog-eared books, and a larger pot of flowers with purple and pink blossoms decorated the bedside table. To shed light into the otherwise dark room, she parted the shades over the balcony door.

"These only require partial light. Direct light can damage them," River explained. She picked up a fuchsia flower with a sunny yellow center and handed it to him. "Here."

"You're a little orchid crazy, aren't you?" Zac teased.

"A friend of mine started the addiction," she admitted.

"A boyfriend?" he ventured.

"No, nothing like that. My roommate Marcy was always collecting plants, and when we'd go to the store and see them, we had this inside joke. Like we were rescuing kittens from the pound or something. We'd each buy one. Just last year, she gave me a pair of these from a trip she took to the islands." River frowned. Her friend had moved away to those islands since then, after striking the Boyfriend Jackpot and reeling in a billionaire—not that the wealth mattered. What she envied most was that Marcy had a spectacular man who loved her, even if that man was a dragon.

"Sounds like you two were close."

"We were. She used to do the photo shoots for my covers. We didn't keep up much after I moved here. She stayed in Houston, and another friend of ours took my room…" River sighed. That friend had also married a billionaire dragon shifter. What were the odds? "Anyway, she lives on an island in the Yucatán now, so she may as well be a million miles away."

"You know, the great thing about photographs is they can be sent online. I bet she has access to all sorts of island hotties."

"Her husband is gorgeous," River agreed, grinning. "I don't think she'd like the thought of a bunch of readers fanning themselves over him, though."

She wandered down the shelf of potted orchids, then plucked another specimen with golden petals. "I want you to take this one too."

The dimple in his cheek returned, tempting her to kiss it and the rest of his handsome face. Good looks like his should have been outlawed. "Why two?" he asked.

"One for your living room, the other for your desk."

"You don't have to do that, River."

"I know, but one orchid is a sad and lonely orchid."

"But they'll be in different rooms."

"Let's pretend they have plant telepathy." She twisted around and plucked up a bar of soap in a cardboard box. Disturbing it released the scent of sandalwood, myrrh, and a little cinnamon into the air. "And here's something for your sensitive nose. I didn't sell this one last time I opened my stall at the farmer's market, so I think it was meant for you," she teased.

Zacarias's warm laugh raised goose bumps on her skin. "Thanks." He sniffed the soap and raised both brows. "Hey, that does smell good. Now tell me what to do with these plants so they aren't dead in a month."

They both laughed, and after she gave him a quick lesson in their care, Zac returned to his side of the duplex. Grinning all the while as she shut the door, River decided to pop by for a "welfare check" on the two orchids in a few days—an excuse to be in his company again.

Upon deciding to enjoy some relaxation after a good deed well done, she returned to her bedroom and gazed out the window overlooking the backyard. Her greenhouse was small, six by eight foot with three levels. Beside it, her small pond flourished with lily pads and aquatic plants. The water pump created a tranquil *whoosh* sound along with the rhythmic splatter of water surging from the fountain.

Her fingers slid over the polished tiger's eye pendant, and within moments of envisioning the kitty in her mind, a rich coat of black fur covered the witch's body. She lowered to four paws and shrank, becoming graceful, surefooted, and sleek.

Slipping out the upper window through a hidden flap cut into the screen, she jumped onto a tree branch and scrambled down the trunk, landing on the fence between the two rear yards.

The duplex sat at the edge of a hundred-acre wood, reminding her of Pooh Bear but lacking the animals full of stuffin'. On breezy days, she sprawled amidst the meadow flowers and enjoyed the sensation of the wind through her fur. Sometimes she explored the deep woods and foraged in her feline body to discover difficult-to-find plants. The best, purest, and healthiest specimens could be found only a few miles from home, it just sometimes took a smaller body to maneuver through the woods where they grew.

And sometimes she wasted a day napping to unwind and recuperate after a stressful week of balancing work-related responsibilities. During those moments, she grew closer to the guardian spirit who granted her special gift.

Witches like River who took an animal shape didn't choose their other form—the Spirit chose them based on their personality after days of ritual and prayer. She had been a cat since she was eighteen and decided shapeshifting was the school of magic she wanted to study. Some witches devoted their lives to becoming masters of deciphering prophetic symbols. Other practitioners chose to advance their skill in brewing potions and the alchemic arts. And then there were witches like River who wanted to walk on the wild side. She considered herself a double major, favoring two types of magic too much to choose.

While it had been a difficult road to follow, she didn't regret it.

She lazed the first hour away in a patch of sunlight on the rim of the pond. The clear afternoon sky eventually lured her from the yard into the shaded swathe of trees. Ball moss clung to the thick oaks, and she surrendered to feline instinct by batting a few leaves fallen to the ground.

The snap of a dry twig echoed through the forest like a gunshot. Abandoning her game, she darted beneath a cluster of upraised tree roots before looking back toward the sound. Occasionally, she saw a fox or bear—even a bald eagle flew overhead once—but never in her wildest imagination did she expect the magnificent creature slinking out from between the trees. Sleek and muscled, the fearless black jaguar prowled forward along the winding path.

Oh shit, oh shit. River froze, crouched low and hoping the sparse grass blades concealed her. Every muscle tensed as she prepared to bolt. *What the hell is a panther doing in town?*

Someone's illegal exotic must have broken free, or worse, been set loose by an irresponsible owner. The closest zoo was in San Antonio, and while it was a possible escapee, it wasn't probable. She would have heard about it on the news.

The panther lifted his face into the breeze then snapped his head toward River. She couldn't run, body paralyzed with fear and muscles uncooperative. Trembling, she tried to will her legs to move.

If she fled, the predator would no doubt give chase. If she remained, he'd probably eat her anyway. And if she transformed, in the few seconds of disorientation following the spell, he'd be upon her in an instant.

Blessed Lady Hecate, please let him move on without harm, she prayed.

The big cat didn't stray from his path. He continued toward her.

Is it a trial? A test?

River considered reverting from her wild, feline shape to two legs, but the panther emanated a sense of peace.

Recognition glittered in his inquisitive, golden-green eyes, and with each passing second, her fear dwindled. This wasn't a creature preparing to make a meal of its prey—if he wanted to eat her, she'd be dead by now. She certainly wouldn't be pondering whether or not he posed a danger.

He came closer, unaware of her internal debate. Trembling, she waited until he closed the remaining distance and put them nose to nose. Her heart slammed in her small chest the whole time his whiskers tickled her face and they breathed each other's air.

I'm smooching a big kitty. A big kitty is smooching me!

Determined to hold her ground in the face of danger, River held eye contact, fascinated by the golden hue and vibrant ring of green. He nuzzled her, and her giggles became a content purr.

The panther bounded ahead a few steps, then looked back over his brawny shoulder. The tip of his tail twitched. When River pounced at it, the game of chase began. Although he had to be the quicker between the two of them, he held back and waited for her to close in on him again. The run carried them in and out of the trees then out to the meadow.

Bumblebees buzzed from flower to flower and a cool breeze whispered through the leaves. Her feline friend stretched out across a sun-warmed spot in the grass. His long legs stuck out in front of him, and then his tail wiggled as he raised his head to peek at her. She accepted the silent invitation and snuggled in against his lean frame.

He smelled unnaturally good for a wild creature, like fresh grass and sandalwood. The scent tickled her memory, familiar and welcoming. Drowsily, she batted his nose with one paw.

His exhaled breaths carried rumbling purrs. The sound lulled River to sleep, and by the time she awakened, her newfound friend had wandered away. The scent of him remained in the grass, a memory of their afternoon playtime together and proof she hadn't hallucinated the entire thing.

***

The next afternoon, River visited her mentor to share her story and ask for advice. They met for a picnic in the rear garden overlooking the pasture. With the smell of the clover and lavender surrounding them, River inhaled her sandwich and babbled every detail of the past three days.

"To top things off, I passed two fender benders on the way here, and some jerk tailgated me down the whole highway," River grumbled.

Pythia gazed through her instead of commenting.

Must be another absence seizure, River thought.

The vacant stare continued, and then the older witch's lips parted. "Double, double, toil and bubble. Fire burn and cauldron bubble."

"Excuse me?"

Awareness returned to Pythia's eyes, and the vacant expression ended. "Hm? I didn't say anything, dear. I was considering your encounter with the panther and your neighbor's ex."

"Yes you did." Pursing her lips, River ran her mentor's words through her head a few times. Pythia had a reputation for prophetic mutterings during her seizures. They sometimes manifested as quotes from famous speeches, or most recently, lines from poetry and plays.

The older witch chuckled. "Perhaps it was one of my moments. Regardless, I think you should keep a close eye on your boy toy before his ex steals him out from under you. Love potions aren't fun and games."

"I know they're not fun and games. Give me some credit. I can't warn him about what I saw without sounding like I was watching through his kitchen windows. I can't reveal I'm also the cat he wants to take in."

"I don't know how you can do it, but what I do know is, if an irresponsible witch plans to screw with the natural balance of things, you *must* intervene. Not only because you like him, but be—"

"Because it's the right thing to do," River finished with a sigh. Biting her lower lip, she watched Pythia spread jam over the still warm bread. She'd left it in the oven a little too long, and jam with an excess of butter was the only cure to soften the tough exterior.

Cure. The answer to her dilemma came to her in a flash of genius. Had that been the message Pythia's subconscious wanted to share? That she needed to fight potion with potion?

"Pythia, I need your help to make a curative potion. If she's tried once, she'll try again, and I want to be ready."

"Sweetheart, unless you're there to pour it down his throat before he dicks her, it's not going to do him any good."

"What can I give him that'll prevent her potion from working? Isn't there a preventative of any kind?"

"Let's consult the book then, shall we?"

They emptied their tea mugs and finished the sandwiches before hurrying inside to Pythia's brewing room. River envied the generous space dedicated to her craft and wished she had more talent with creating delicate and potent concoctions. Her potions were straightforward and blunt, with strong earthy tastes she couldn't mask.

Wooden shelves spanned the walls in rows of three. Color coded opaque jars held sensitive reagents, and plastic storage units contained packages of dried goods in Ziploc baggies and wrapped in linen. She had four brewing stations, one of which was a repurposed slow cooker for simmering certain mixtures.

Pythia used the closet to store racks of drying herbs from her garden.

"I need a dedicated alchemy room," River muttered. "I'm jealous every time I come in here."

"There's no need to be jealous. You know Daddy said he'd help you if you ever decide to set up your spare bedroom."

"I know, I know. I just feel bad pulling him away from his relaxing retirement to do strenuous labor at my place. He never accepts money either."

"Are you kidding me? Dad is bored. He needs to keep active, River. It'll do him good to have something to do besides read papers on the porch and reminisce about the good old days of when Atropos had a population of two hundred people and no crime."

Was there crime now? River chuckled. "Fine. You've convinced me. Maybe I'll develop some skills if I have the space to collect more ingredients and really get to work."

"I'll give him a call after you solve your romance problem. And you shouldn't be so hard on yourself. Your potions are brilliant, and you hardly need my help. Honestly, you're harder on yourself than you should be."

"My potions stink," River muttered under her breath.

Her friend stood on tiptoe to remove a thick, leather-bound book from one of the high shelves. She was a cute thing, like a wee sprite in a green, triple-layered circle skirt and a black, sleeveless midriff top. Her silver-streaked blonde hair fell to her butt and must have weighed as much as she did.

"That book looks like it weighs fifty pounds. Mine isn't nearly that big."

"Thank you! I still remember the day I made it four hundred years ago. Or was it five hundred? I forget," she replied. Pythia was one of those witches who had been reincarnated so many times she no longer kept count. She blew the dust from the cover and set it on a table, and then they began to turn through the pages. The contents read in another language River didn't recognize, the script ancient and unidentifiable.

"Here. It says the bezoar of a unicorn will curb lustful thoughts." She clapped in victory, jangling a dozen spell-imbued bangles on her wrists and arms. "I forgot all about that."

"I don't want to curb his lustful thoughts and rob him of his personality. He's a flirtatious guy."

"Right, we don't want to do that, but given crushed in a solution containing marshmallow and these other ingredients, you'll have an elixir that'll only negate the enchantment. If he's a randy guy, he'll still be hot for you and anyone else with a pair of tits."

"You're a genius."

"Of course."

"Where'd you get unicorn stuff anyway?"

Pythia's cheeks dimpled when she smiled, but there was sadness to the expression. "A friend. Unicorns are giving folk, and when they die, they have preferences."

"Yeah?"

"They're the world's first organ donors. It's a little morbid, but they'd rather save a few lives than have a Viking's funeral or waste in the earth."

The idea twisted River's stomach as much as it touched her heart. "That's sweet and, uh, a little macabre. I know they have healing properties and all but…"

"What? Did you think we just found unicorn horns lying around? That they shed them and grew another like deer losing their antlers?"

River pinched Pythia's arm. "Smartass. I never considered it, okay?"

An impromptu potions lesson began with Pythia guiding her through the steps. She learned shortcuts along the way and beamed with pride when the simmering brew released a fragrant, sweet aroma up to her on thin tendrils of steam and smoke.

"That smells divine," Pythia encouraged. "Two more stirs, clockwise, then allow it rest. You'll know it's ready once it's formed a protective film."

An hour later, they had a bell jar filled with pale pink elixir. A few drops of the potent restorative would negate any potion affecting mental faculties.

"What about my big cat in the forest? Do you have any advice about *that*?"

Pythia raised a shoulder, shrugging. "Could have been a shifter. I wouldn't dwell on it, love. Stranger things have happened in Atropos."

"Yeah, like vampires. Ever since you told me there's a coven house nearby, I get the willies at night whenever I'm alone."

Pythia waved her hand in a dismissive gesture. "The bloodsuckers of Rosenhaven keep to themselves, and they're more afraid of us than we should be of them. Now you said something about a fender bender, right? Well, more than cars and a little road rage are involved in this now. Isaac Lawrence shot his neighbor's pit bull two nights ago for the mere crime of getting loose and shredding the trash again."

River's heart sank, and tears sprang to her eyes. She loved dogs, even if they were usually adorable, drooling idiots. "What? Isaac is as sweet as can be. I know the dog is kind of a menace sometimes, but he's so friendly."

"Exactly. Plus, Isaac's even dog-sat Willard while Rudy was out of town on business over the summer. It was a big fight. Huge. The police had to come take both of them away."

The news about Willard's murder changed things. Usually the summer heat came with increased aggression and verbal altercations, but the recent days in central Texas had been cool and temperate. Summer had ended, autumn sweeping in fair, cloudy days meant for lounging on the porch with sweet tea or lavender lemonade.

So what the hell was going on in Atropos to turn neighbor against neighbor in the most heartbreaking way?

CHAPTER 3

A couple of days became a week as River struggled over the conflicting signs. She read the stars, tea leaves, and even tried to divine with Oracle cards, but each method revealed a different piece to a larger puzzle.

"What the hell is going on out there?" she wondered.

The cards told her to expect betrayal, heartbreak, and chaos. Death.

Whether they realized it or not, the townspeople felt something big was coming and vacated the streets, drawing their children indoors early. Whenever River inhaled deep, something musty and stale tainted the air, and an unfamiliar buzz of things to come added weight to the atmosphere.

Irritable, she phoned another young witch who lived in Austin, older in spirit but equally youthful in body. She'd been reincarnated once before and had regained most of the memories associated with her past life.

Despite Gloria's experience, the older witches tended to treat her and River the same.

"Hi, River."

"Hey, Gloria. Is now a good time to speak or are you teaching a class?"

"My kindergarten ballet class isn't for another hour. I'm just setting up in the studio now, but I have time to chat. What's up?"

"Have you felt the disturbance?"

Gloria laughed. "Who hasn't?"

"Did the circle assign you the task of interpreting it too?"

"Yeah. My local group has been meeting every Friday night to combine our efforts."

"But no luck."

"It's like peering into fog," Gloria said.

River blew out a disappointed breath, tossing a curl out of her face. "I can't tell if it's demonic in origin or dark magic."

"No one can. You know it's bad when the *ancient* crones conscript the rest of us into doing their work. Even Grace and Pythia are stumped."

They spent a few more minutes discussing an art project for Gloria's dance recital at the start of summer— River had promised to design a backdrop for the production—then said their goodbyes and hung up.

"What the hell could it be?" she questioned the empty room while thoughtfully tapping her lower lip with her index finger. She gazed out the window while sitting cross-legged on the living room floor.

Only one possibility occurred to her, but heavy doubts made her hesitant to bring them up. She stared down at her phone, chewing on her lip, then hit the call button. Pythia answered on the third ring.

"River, did we have plans today?" her friend's voice greeted her in confusion.

"No, not for today," she assured her. Although Pythia was a wise witch, her epilepsy could make her scatterbrained at times, enough to forget appointments if she didn't pencil them into a calendar. "Actually, I was calling to run a thought past you."

"Oh, of course. What did you need, dear?"

"Is it possible we could be dealing with a black coven? I mean, that's the only reason I can think of for being blocked like this. It's like a… a…"

"Smokescreen? Yes, I'd begun to wonder the same," her mentor said. "There hasn't been a grudge of witches since the Great Depression."

Those had been dark times, a worldwide period of economic and magical devastation when dark witches had banded together and preyed on the needy. They'd taken sacrifices from the desperate and enslaved the misguided who made foolish deals with them in exchange for prosperity.

River shuddered when she thought about it. Of course, she hadn't been born then, but most witches studied history so it wouldn't be repeated. A grudge, the term for a gang of evil witches, couldn't be more accurate. Once a human made the mistake of crossing one, they usually dropped off the face of the planet.

"What happens if it *is* a black coven?"

Pythia sighed. "Then we'll have to tread carefully. If it *is* a black coven, they'll be led by a powerful warlock, and their dark nature alone isn't enough to take any direct action. Free will and all that. They're allowed to worship who they choose, even if it is the likes of Lilith or Kali."

River grunted. Warlocks didn't exist in the Wiccan religion, but to magical practitioners like her, they were terrifying leaders in the black arts who encouraged their flock to honor and pray to dark spirits. "I get that they're allowed to worship who they want, but clearly they're up to no good if there's enough magic in the air to give most of us bad dreams. If there is a warlock around, he or she can't be innocent."

A pause hung between them before the older witch said in a gentle voice, "You're the only one to experience bad dreams, River. Regardless, nightmares caused from negative magical energy isn't a violation of our principles either."

Only her? For the first time since the dismal atmosphere had spread over Atropos, River felt a strange stirring in her gut. "What about the aggression? They're causing people to fight each other."

"We'd have to prove intent. Negative energy can be a byproduct of even common day spells. Regardless, I'll inform the circle of your thoughts, as well as mine. If we are dealing with black witches, then it will take a coordinated effort between all our covens to suss them out. In the meantime, let me know if you sense anything else. And, River?"

"Yeah?"

"Good work. For what it's worth, I'm proud of you for figuring that out."

***

Lucia arrived the next day while River poured birdseed for the finches outside. She and Zacarias each kept a couple of feeders for the songbirds, finches, and hummingbirds, and divided the responsibility of refilling them.

Across the yard in his driveway, Zacarias toiled beneath his car. He performed most of his maintenance and upkeep on the sleek sports car.

River heard him groan from yards away when his ex's sporty coupe slid into the drive behind him. He came out from beneath the car and wiped oil-stained hands on his jeans.

"What do you want?"

"Is that any way to greet me? I came to be nice and bring you things you left behind in the storage we rented."

"Yeah, okay. Thanks. Where are they?"

"They're in the trunk, but wait, I brought this as a peace offering. You know, to apologize for what happened last time." Lucia reached through the driver's window to remove an enormous glass bottle. Squinting from afar, River recognized the label of an expensive tequila brand. The sheer volume and name must have cost Lucia over a hundred bucks. Maybe two hundred.

"No thanks," Zac replied.

Yes!

Shameless, River eavesdropped and took her time with the bird feeders, sitting back to watch the finches before heading inside. It didn't take long for Zacarias to chase his ex-wife away. He retrieved his belongings from her trunk then retreated inside after a terse thank you. Lucia's incredulous expression was priceless.

Two days later, she arrived with coffee over the weekend while River tended to her sage garden. The witch beamed proudly about how she remembered his preferred flavor and asked if he'd help with a few last-minute touch-ups before the big inspection at their home.

Zacarias argued with her in the lawn and reluctantly agreed. He returned later in the evening in a poor mood, definitely not how a guy would behave after banging his afternoon away. River surprised him with brownies and chai tea, both sweetened with the elixir.

Despite Lucia's attempts to pollute his drinks with potion, River found excuses to feed him snacks and drinks every day, sometimes twice a day to build the prophylactic antidote up in his system. Lucia would create a reason to drive over and try to poison Zac with lust-inducing tonics, and River cheerfully watched her dismayed expressions whenever he sent her packing after they completed their business.

He was really too nice of a guy to humor her.

One afternoon, River caught Lucia studying the herb garden she had planted out in the front yard. River knelt in the flower bed several feet away, planting pansies, and tensed when the woman shot her a considering look.

"What are you doing?" she asked.

"Adding some flowers for the upcoming winter. Pansies are great this time of the year."

Lucia pressed her lips together in a disapproving line. Her eyes traveled over the bunches of barely tamed pineapple sage, the sprigs of lavender, and the generous peppermint spilling from oversized containers. "Our garden was better."

Before River could respond, Lucia spun on a pencil-thin heel and stalked to her car. The tires squealed as she burned away down the road.

"Don't pay her any attention," Zac said, chuckling. "I think I put her in a shitty mood."

"Yeah, I noticed. I was totally an innocent bystander here."

"Well, I think it looks amazing. What my catty ex-wife didn't say was that she hired a landscaper to do all the hard work for her while she sipped a daiquiri from a lounge chair nearby. You know, in her best bikini."

River laughed at the picture his words painted.

"Wanna watch the game with me after you're finished with that?"

"Sure. I'm down for that. Who we rooting for?" she asked.

"Does it matter? American football sucks. Inviting you over for sports is just an excuse to bask in your beauty and drink beer together."

The compliment warmed her face with pleasure. "In that case, since we both hate American football, make it anime or a horror movie and I'm game."

"You're on."

CHAPTER 4

Z acarias stretched his arms over his head and leaned to one side then the next. His back popped. After sitting for six hours at his desk, he was ready to get out of the office and run wild through the leaf-strewn wilderness behind his house.

"I'll finish this code up at home, Harrison. Maybe I'll even try to convince River to do a mock-up for you to look at."

His friend nodded. The resemblance between Harrison and his father, the company's owner, was close enough to fool strangers into believing they were twins. They both had the same dark hair and fair skin. And of course, they both shifted into ravens. "Thanks, man. She's done some great work."

Years ago, Zac had worked as a mere programmer for his friend until he broke free to pursue launching his own independent company. Now they'd joined forces to develop the ultimate video game, a dream come true with the potential for making them both richer than ever and getting their work into a million hands.

"I'll let her know what you said."

An enormous grin spread over Harrison's face. "Over drinks, right? When are you gonna hit that, dude?"

"Hard to romance a woman when the ex keeps dropping by for stupid, ridiculous shit."

Harrison grimaced. "She's still bugging you?"

"Yeah. If there's an excuse, Lucia has used it."

"Dude, tell her to shove off."

"You think I don't? It's like she's got radar or something. Any time I think about going over to put the moves on River, Lucia's ass is right there in my face with a bottle of booze or something."

His friend shrugged. "She wants that D, man. You have nobody to blame but yourself for that. Want me to call Drakenstone back to deal with her?"

"Nah. I can handle Lucia, but thanks. Besides, having a dragon around weirds me out."

"Your choice, man, but the offer stands. Anyway, good luck. Sounds like you need it."

Zac grunted and shut down his computer. With his luck, he'd drive home to find Lucia staked out on his porch with another list of bullshit excuses.

Harrison had a point though. For as long as he'd been admiring and checking out his neighbor, he'd done nothing to make good on it.

Inspired by their conversation, he took the long route home to enjoy the scenic countryside of rural Texas, and then swung by a Sonic Drive-In when he entered Atropos. The tiny town of 2000 had been named after the Greek goddess of fate by the founders.

The reason why never intrigued him enough to look up the town's history, but years of living in Texas had taught him it wasn't the strangest name on the census in their state. Somewhere to the south, there was a place named Friendship, Texas. And to the east, Quickdraw was home to some of the scariest shifters around.

"Here's your order, Mr. Silva."

A teenaged waitress handed him a sack of burgers and shakes through the drive-thru window.

If he knew River, and he was pretty sure he did by now, she'd be at her computer while a movie droned in the background, oblivious to the late hour of the evening, and it was long past time for her to eat a decent meal. Maybe burgers, tots, and strawberry cream shakes weren't the best of suppers, but he wanted to butter her up prior to commissioning her talent.

Before Zac had the chance to set his order in the passenger seat, the car behind him honked. The driver laid on the horn and leaned out the window, flipping up his middle finger. The waitress frowned and shot Zac an apologetic look.

"Good luck," he murmured before pulling forward.

As a bad feeling brewed in his gut, Zac took his time in the parking lot. He peered in his rearview mirror in time to see the jerk behind him hurling an enormous forty-four-ounce drink back at the waitress. Without taking a moment to think about what he was doing, he threw his car in park. He jumped out, and in a couple bounds, came up to the passenger side of the car.

"Hey, man, is that really called for?" Zac looked across the car at the crying waitress. She had dark soda splashed all over her face, hair, and clothes. "You all right?"

Another employee came up with napkins and tried to help the girl dry her face.

"Stupid bitch can't even get a soda order right. I said diet, not regular," the man in the car raged.

"Dude, it's soda. She could have dispensed another one for you."

"Fuck you, pretty boy. You don't run my life."

Already pissed at the treatment of the girl, Zac put a threatening tone in his voice. "Look, if you have a problem with me calling you out for douchebag behavior, why don't you get out of the car and do something?"

The man peeled away from the drive, barely missing Zac's car.

"That motherf—" He bit his tongue and growled, but another sob from the waitress brought his mind away from the dark thoughts starting to brew. *You know what? I'm cool. He's not worth that kind of anger.*

"I'm so sorry about that," she babbled.

"Hey, it's not your fault. Did he pay for his food at least?" Zac asked. The girl shook her head, so he passed her a twenty from his wallet. "Keep the change and give the police his plate number. Throwing a drink at you constitutes battery."

A young man with a tag identifying him as the shift manager stepped up. "Thanks, Mr. Silva."

"No problem."

They tried to reimburse him for his meal, but he waved them off and headed back to his car. The entire way home he wondered about the odd encounter. Soda hardly seemed worth getting enraged over.

Once Zac turned down his street, he passed a pair of kids trotting by on their ponies.

"Hi, Mr. Silva!" one of them called.

He waved back to them and smiled. At least kids still had their manners and weren't falling prey to the weird epidemic of assholery infecting Atropos. He cruised by them and to the end of the street. True to expectation, the front window of River's side revealed her through the parted blinds, her features highlighted by the glowing monitor.

Just as he killed the ignition, Lucia's car pulled up behind him in the drive.

"Like clockwork," he muttered under his breath, wondering about his unfortunate luck. Obviously, someone up there had it out for him.

Deep breath. If you can handle six years of marriage, you can handle her for five more minutes.

Zac stepped out of the car, calm and prepared to wrangle Satan back into her car.

"Perfect timing," Lucia called. Her black stilettos clicked against the asphalt as she approached. "I have that paperwork you asked for, plus a little something extra."

He grunted. "You could have had the lawyer fax them for me to review." His eyes dropped to the "something" extra cradled in her arms. She held a bottle of Chilean red, one of the few labels he liked. What the hell was up with her always trying to bribe him with booze?

"We can hardly celebrate over the phone, Zacarias. Don't be silly."

Five minutes, he reminded himself. "Fine. Come on in. Let's get it over and done with."

He made Lucia wait while he handled his outside chores. He fetched the paper from the end of the drive, grabbed his UPS package on the porch, and crossed behind the house to the water outlet. Shamelessly, he turned on the sprinklers without warning his interrupting ex.

Pssst pssst pssst, the spritzing water hissed in a relaxed rhythm. Prompt squeals told him he'd been successful.

When he came around to the front again, the black cat approached from the direction of River's home. He dipped down and plucked her up for an affectionate snuggle.

The smell Zac associated with River, warm vanilla and sugar, assaulted him as the kitty rubbed her face against his jaw. Her whiskers tickled his throat, followed by a pleased purr.

River must have taken her in and fed her.

"Ugh. Leave that mangy thing outside." Lucia pushed through the doorway the moment he unlocked it.

"Sorry, *gata*, best you stay outside for a few. We'll play later, I promise." When he tried to set her on the wooden porch chair, the cat dug her claws into his shirt and refused to budge. "Hey, I promise I'll be back for you in a few."

"New girlfriend?" Lucia smirked over her shoulder. "You can do better."

"Cats always trump snakes, Lucia."

He tossed the fast food order on the counter and set the melting shakes in the freezer. Lucia helped herself to the kitchen where she opened and poured the wine while he scanned the paperwork she'd dropped on the couch. Neon-colored tabs marked each spot requiring his signature.

Distrusting her, he scrutinized each line and read every word. "Why are these asking for a signature when I asked for a copy to review? Maybe I should call Doug—"

"Do you honestly think I'd cheat you?" she asked.

Zac stared.

"Okay, maybe you do, but what the hell do I have to gain from it now when I want to make things better between us? I miss your friendship."

"Don't we need a notary or something to witness this?" he asked.

"Possibly, but I'll make sure it's all taken care of. I'm friends with the realtor."

Meow. Meow.

The cat pawed at the sliding glass door. Poor thing probably wanted a snack, but he didn't trust Lucia to keep her cool if another accident occurred. He sipped wine and flipped through the final pages. Everything appeared to be in order, and for the sake of rushing Lucia out of his house, he needed a pen. If she wanted to cheat him, she was more than welcome if it meant he never had to see her on his doorstep again.

"Here." Lucia offered a fancy ballpoint from her purse.

"Thanks." *She looks good. And she smells great.* The random thought slithered across his mind as he picked up subtle notes of rose and something exotic but unfamiliar. Floral. Roving his gaze up Lucia's long legs, Zac found himself struck with the sudden urge to discover what color panties she wore beneath her sleek business suit. He imagined flimsy, crotchless silk trimmed with lace over her usual Brazilian wax. Then she uncrossed and crossed her legs again, providing the answer.

None.

"There." He cleared his throat and pushed the thick file toward her. "Everything is signed."

"Then a toast is in order, don't you think?"

Their glasses clinked together. "To selling the house." *And being free,* he added in silence. The property had been the last thing tying them together. *So glad we never had kids.*

Warmth filled his belly with the next sip of wine, accompanied by a wave of nostalgia. He and Lucia had enjoyed some good times in that house, even planned to have a child once she cemented her position with the modeling agency.

His tongue betrayed him. "I miss you," he blurted.

Lucia paused mid sip then lowered the glass to the table. Her gray eyes widened with interest. "How much?"

Draining the glass didn't help his parched mouth, but it freed his hands. In his desperate haste to stand, he toppled the kitchen chair over sideways, and before the next thump of his racing heart, he dragged Lucia into his arms. He twisted her hair around one fist, anchoring her for a desperate kiss. Each second became more demanding than the last.

Wine flavored her lips, and her perfume surrounded him, overwhelming his senses. The animal inside him demanded satisfaction. It craved a deeper, more intimate contact.

Zac's resolve wavered, then shattered and broke.

One firm tug pulled her skirt around her waist, exposing slim thighs and her bare bottom to his touch. He squeezed a handful, relishing the warmth of her in his palm. Too long had passed since he claimed her body.

"Gimme a second to find a rubber, Luce."

"We don't need a condom," she breathed against his lips. "I'm clean, baby. You know that."

"You still on the pill?"

"Mm-hmm."

Her fingers slid over his groin, tracing the zipper until she received a reaction. "Fuck," he groaned out loud, jerking his jeans open. Her warm hand slipped beneath the waistband.

"Missed me? Missed the way my mouth feels on you?"

"Yes… yes."

Lucia's fingers slid around him and glided back and forth, jerking to a casual rhythm. Hard as a branding iron, he ached for the familiar cradle of her body.

The doorbell chime startled him, but Lucia leaned in to kiss him again. "Ignore it," she murmured.

The doorbell buzzed again, his insistent visitor laying on the button.

"Go get in the bed upstairs." He squeezed her again then nudged her toward the stairs.

"But—"

"Strip and wait for me in bed. You know how I like it."

After a quick repositioning, he fastened his jeans and cracked open the door, using it as his shield.

"Look, dude, you don't gotta press the damned button so many ti—" River's worried expression came into view when he peered outside onto the porch, brows wrinkled and lip caught between her teeth. "River?"

"Hey, Zac. Uh, I'm sorry to bother you, but… um… I need to see you for a minute."

"Now's not the best time. I kinda have company."

"I know, and I'm *really* sorry, but my computer glitched up, and I have a deadline for this project. I misread an email, and I didn't realize Sassy needed a cover for the new book *tomorrow*… It's all my fault, and I can't forgive myself if I screw up her release." She plucked one of her dark curls, twisting it around her index finger. "I'll pay you."

"Zac?" Lucia called from upstairs.

Everything in his head became mush. He couldn't concentrate on anything but the intoxicating smell of Lucia's arousal, the taste of her lips still on his tongue reminding him of how much he needed to drive into her *now*.

He wanted to make River happy. He wanted to screw Lucia. He wanted to share dinner with his friendly neighbor. He wanted to dick his ex-wife until she was crippled. Conflicting emotions ebbed and flowed like the tide, practically tearing him in two.

Why am I gonna sleep with Lucia? he wondered in a fleeting moment of clarity. It faded. *Because she deep throats like no one's business, that's why.*

"Please, Zac. I swear it'll only take a minute, and I'll owe you. I'll even help with your upcoming promotional stuff. I'll make time in my schedule."

River's one of the best artists I've ever seen when she dabbles in illustration. Unable to pass up the opportunity, he stepped onto the small front stoop and pulled the door shut. "Yeah, okay. I'll have a look at it."

He followed her across the cool pavement and damp grass to her side of the duplex. Rain scented the air, but he didn't recall an early-evening shower, too distracted with matters inside, like rushing Lucia out of his house. The fresh air whipped against his cheeks and calmed the lust down a notch, allowing him to concentrate on something besides sex with the ex-wife he'd barely tolerated minutes ago.

Zac cleared his throat as he stepped in behind his neighbor. Spicy incense wafted from a nearby censer shaped like a kitten. "So what happened?"

"I spilled my tea and must have hit something when I was cleaning it all up. I lost the files I was working on."

River hovered over his shoulder while he took a seat at her computer and started to work. "I should be able to recover them. Give me a few minutes, all right?"

"Thanks, Zac, I mean it. You want anything?"

"Huh? No, I'm good."

She paced behind him and wrung her hands a few times, cracking her knuckles and glancing at the clock. "Are you sure I can't get you anything?"

A break, maybe. Of all the nights to bother me. Lucia was in his bed, ready and waiting. Probably pissed too, which meant rough sex was waiting for him upon his return. The pleasant thought urged him to work as fast as he was able, grunting in response to River's silly questions.

Silly questions? Wasn't River the one he wanted to dine with in the first place?

***

The stink of Lucia's perfume swarmed all over Zac, and thankfully, as a woman, River was immune. The other witch had tailored it specifically to him, and the preventative elixir hadn't worked.

His ex had sunk to a new low, finally fed up enough with River's cock-blocking to use another form of enchantment—the kind of enchantment that was forbidden by their laws, a dozen times powerful than the average lust potion. Everything River had ever learned about dark magic told her Lucia had consorted with a demon.

While Zac worked his virtual magic to save her "lost" file, she wondered how the hell she'd keep him away from the seductress next door. Although it was an unnecessary, fabricated dilemma, his skill impressed her. Deliberately corrupting the file had been the only plan she could come up with to get him away from his potion-dealing ex-wife. She kept back-ups of her work safely tucked away on a flash drive.

"There you are. Good as new. Anyway, I'll see you tomorrow." He rose from the desk and turned to face her, but his distracted gaze flickered toward the front door.

Now or never.

Finding her courage, she stepped forward and hooked one arm around Zac's shoulders. She yanked him down and tilted her face up to meet his descending mouth. He resisted at first, cold and unyielding, as confused as he was ensorcelled by the other witch's magic. The scent of Lucia's concoction flavored his lips, and just as River thought it was time to give up, they parted. His tongue advanced into her mouth, tentative then exploring.

She had to get his mind off Lucia. She had to break the attraction for at least a few minutes longer. If she released him too soon, it would all revert, and then Zac would spend his night balls deep in his ex-wife and up shit creek without a paddle.

River wasn't sure making out with him would break the spell, but she had to try something.

"What was that about?" Zac asked when they parted, voice breathless and strained with need.

"Um… thank you?"

"That's one hell of a thank you."

"I've, uh, actually wanted to do that for a while," she admitted.

"Good."

Kisses like his should have been illegal. Trapping River between the wall and his hard body, Zacarias plundered her mouth again with his skillful tongue and firm lips. She may have initiated it, but she surrendered and passed the lead to him. He'd haunted her dreams enough that finally acting on them was a relief.

Encouraged by her palms gliding up and down his chest to knead the firm muscles, Zac tugged her leg up to his hip and ground against her. Her heart slammed in her chest as she gained an intimate awareness of his athletic frame, learning him inch by inch.

"Zac?"

"Hm?"

"You have a guest at your place."

He chuckled low and warm against her cheek and nibbled her ear. "She'll leave." His voice was oddly bemused, back to his usual self without the distracted tone of a man under an enchantment.

Somehow, she'd broken a lust potion with a kiss. The other witches wouldn't believe her if she told them.

"Is that what you want?" she asked. "I mean… she comes by an awful lot to be only an ex."

Why wouldn't her heart stop racing?

Zacarias sighed and laid his cheek atop her head. "It's funny, you know. I was beginning to wonder the same thing. Sometimes when Lucia shows up, I miss her. I regret going through with the divorce and want her back… Then it's like my head's clear again, and I remember all the money she took me for, along with the lies and the cheating."

Testing him, she persisted. "You were married a long time."

"Six years. That's not so long."

"Six years longer than I've been married," she retorted.

"She's only buzzing around now that the company is making money hand over fist. I think she regrets the split."

Excellent. She had broken it after all. And while he was in no danger of returning to his sordid activities with Lucia, neither of them moved. She waited for Zac to release her, and likewise, he seemed to expect her to pull away. She shifted until her ear was above his heart to hear the powerful, tranquil thump of its rhythm.

"I read about the recent success in the news. Congrats."

"Thanks." Zac quieted and held her longer, the silence broken only by a discreet sniff.

Had he just smelled her hair?

"Zac?"

Snapping out of whatever trance he'd gone into, Zac broke free and stepped back. "You're right though. I better kick her out before she makes herself at home."

"Okay. Um… I'm free after, if you want."

"I thought you had a cover?"

Shit! "I… it's actually, um, almost done. You saved me having to start over."

"Gotcha. Anyway, this'll just take a sec."

River led him to the front door while hoping he'd shower Lucia's stink off him after he kicked the harpy to the curb. Once he was gone, she sprinted upstairs to her room. The spacious bay window in the master bedroom had sold the house, so to speak, and overlooked the front yard with a fantastic view of their humble street. From the moment she saw it, the place was hers.

Well… theirs, in a way, since she shared the building with Zac but owned her distinct half.

At first, she strained to hear. After a few moments, the sound of their argument drifted over on the evening breeze.

"What's gotten into you? What do you mean you want me to leave? You can't do this!" Lucia whined in a shrill voice as Zac walked her out to her car.

Technically, she'd have to be using her feet for him to be walking her out to the car, River thought. Zac had picked Lucia up and carried her across the lawn with his hands on her waist while she flailed, kicked, and screamed like an angry toddler.

"I can't make you leave my place?"

"You can't kick me out like some common… some common—"

"I'd finish that sentence for you, but it would be an insult to whores. At least they earn their money," Zac countered.

Lucia's mouth opened and closed like a fish while River snorted into her hands and struggled to keep her laughter private.

"Stay away from me, Lucia. I'll drive the paperwork to the lawyers myself, and we can meet *there*. I'm finished with being civil and understanding. Stay the hell out of my life."

He left his defeated ex at the car.

"Yes!" River pumped a fist in the air and leaped up from the window seat, only to splash dive onto the bed and cackle with laughter. She'd won, and there was no way Zac would allow the leech into his life again for her to make subsequent tries.

Especially after she reported her suspicions to Pythia. As a senior witch, she'd be the next person in the chain of command to take her complaint. If Lucia had consorted with an evil spirit, she'd put their entire sisterhood at risk.

With plans of catching up to him in an hour or so to check in, she heated water for tea and resumed her evening routine. Sharp raps on the front door echoed through the house as she tore open an individual wrapper of fragrant orange spice.

She hurried to the door, flooded with excitement. Part of her hoped Zac had come to finish where they'd left off, but the responsible half knew it was poor timing. Aside from her reluctance to leap into bed for a round of casual sex with a guy, it wouldn't be appropriate while he was coming down off a wicked lust potion.

Or compulsion, she reminded herself. There was more at work there.

River unlocked and opened the door without glancing outside. "Hey, that was fast—"

Torn bits of sage, mugwort, and the newly planted pansies struck River in the face. Lucia glared at her over the threshold.

"You meddling little bitch. What did you do?" She wore a heavy layer of makeup in a flawless, airbrushed mask, but fury spread splotches of red over her throat and upper chest.

River had always figured Zac's ex would catch on. Refusing to succumb to shame for her intervention, she raised her chin and met Lucia's gaze dead on.

"Leveled the playing field. You chased the man off, and now you're trying to violate his mind to get him back. It's wrong."

"If you think you're going to magic him away—"

"I'm not using magic to get him," River cut her off.

"You are. Pretty pathetic too. I've never had to use magic to get a man—"

"Have you ever *had* a man?" Lucia interrupted hotly. Her eyes flashed. "As if any man wants to screw a woman made of pudding and dumplings. Get over yourself. Zacarias and I may have a misunderstanding between us for now, but you're only going to get hurt if you step into my personal business with him again."

Pudding? Before River could retort, Lucia strode away on her ridiculous stiletto heels. River wouldn't be caught dead wearing a pair unless she wanted to resemble a newborn baby calf taking its first steps.

"Don't think I won't be reporting you for what you did today!" she called after Lucia.

As her confidence evaporated, River shut the door and tossed her ramen dinner into the disposal. So much for an evening of empty, cheap calories. She resisted the temptation to angrily binge on the toffee caramel crunch ice cream stashed in her freezer and returned to the living room where she turned on her favorite paranormal television series and pretended to work.

"Not all of us want to starve ourselves or have surgeries and crap," she grumbled. Zac had mentioned paying for at least three of his ex's procedures.

When another series of knocks interrupted her pity party, she shot the door a dirty look as if it had caused offense. Sighing, she ventured over to squint through the stained-glass panel. Zac waited on the other side, casually dressed in a tee and shorts with both hands in his pockets.

River peeked out at him with her body behind the door, afraid he'd only see pudding thighs and a doughy bottom. "Hi."

"Hey."

A few awkward moments passed in silence before Zac finally pushed the door the rest of the way and helped himself inside. "I'm not pissed about you kissing me if that's what the shy act is about."

"I wasn't worried about you being pissed."

"Good."

"Good?"

Zacarias closed the gap between them and pulled her in flush against his body. Her lips parted in anticipation as he claimed her mouth in a possessive, hungry kiss. As if he'd never left, they picked up where the action had ended before. River's heart slammed in her chest, beating faster than a hummingbird's wings. She curled her fingers around Zac's nape, and in return, he cupped her bottom in his large palms and tugged her in closer.

She wasn't sure which of them broke away first. They pressed their cheeks together while they each drew in thirsty breaths.

"I bought dinner for us," Zac said in a low, husky voice. His arms remained in place around her, warm and strong enough to banish any worries wrought by his ex.

"It's not much, but I'd planned to invite you over before she interrupted."

"Okay. Um, gimme a moment to change."

"Why? You look good the way you are."

River glanced down at her shorts and dull gray tank. "I look like a bum."

"Then I do too."

He dragged her out onto the porch. Before she had the chance to warn him that the keys were still inside on the hook, he turned her lock and shut the door behind them.

Shit. She'd have to worry about getting back into her place later.

"Uh, one thing though, before you see it... though judging from how your porch looks *and* smells like an herb storm, you may already know what happened..." Zac sighed and ran his fingers through his air. His sheepish smile, genuine and warm, took the edge off River's anger. "I'm sorry about your flowers."

Refusing to allow Lucia's childishness to ruin her mood, she forced the grim feelings at bay and flashed Zacarias a weak smile. "Not your fault. You can't be responsible for what an adult woman decides to do."

Besides, most of it would grow out again if given tender love and patience.

"Yeah well, let's just say I owe you a lot for your interruption."

As if to make up for it, Zacarias dragged her to the couch once they were inside and handed over the remote. Then he served reheated bacon cheeseburger on thick Texas toast.

Finally. A guy who understands that a girl likes to eat. River wasn't in any danger of wasting away, but for the most part, she enjoyed her diet, her curves, and felt confident about both until a mouthy model had to put her down. In hindsight, she felt stupid for allowing Lucia to impact her at all.

"Mind if I grab some drinks?"

"Knock yourself out. There are shakes in the freezer."

After catching a whiff of tainted wine at the kitchen sink, River tossed the empty bottle in the trash then rinsed out the contaminated glasses. It smelled sour to her, an underlying odor as bitter as the witch who brewed the foul concoction.

"Are you doing my dishes or getting shakes?" Zac bellowed from the living room.

"Why not both?" she murmured under her breath.

Confident she'd destroyed all traces of the nefarious potion, she fetched the half frozen dairy delights and rejoined Zac on the sofa. Her heart swelled with elation the moment he dragged her in against his side, treating her to the masculine and woodsy aroma of the soap she'd gifted him. He must have showered after getting rid of Lucia.

"So…" Her fingers splayed over his chest, stroking over a hard pectoral through his cotton tee. "Did you drink all of the wine before inviting me over?"

He made a face. "Nah, it wasn't any good. Tasted funny. You want booze to go with the milkshake?"

"Maybe…"

"Beer work for you or did you want something stronger?"

"Whatever you have handy."

Zac swiped his thumb over her lower lip, catching a smear of mustard left from the burger. Then he bounded off to the kitchen. River dragged a napkin over her face the moment he was gone.

No matter how hard she tried to come off like a sultry fox, something—like a mouth covered in mustard—always intervened. As least she hadn't dribbled fries down her cleavage this time the way she had on another unfortunate date.

Zac returned a minute later and passed her a tall glass filled with ice and dark liquid. She recognized Coke on the first sip, sweetened with a splash of vanilla and the low burn of alcohol.

"Hey, did you take in that little black cat?" he asked.

River tilted her head up for a look at him and played it cool. "No. Why?"

"Oh. She smelled like your place, so I thought maybe you'd decided to take her in."

"Nah. If I had a pet, it would be the most neglected thing ever."

"I doubt it. Anyway, I'm thinking of keeping her as long as you don't plan to."

Shit. "She's way too healthy looking to be a stray, dude. I think she just likes prowling around the neighborhood."

"Yeah, you're probably right."

"You look disappointed," she ventured cautiously.

"I like cats." He shrugged and polished off his burger.

Over the course of a few hours and several drinks, they watched some movies ranging from supernatural thrillers to action-packed fantasy. All the while, River resisted the naughty thoughts inspired by her fuzzy, alcohol brain. As tempting as it was to bust out of her clothing on the first official date, she had personal standards to uphold.

CHAPTER 5

Thankfully, River didn't have to use magic or call a locksmith to get into her place. With the arrival of fall, the cooler nights and a few wise plant choices combatted the insect population, allowing her to keep the windows cracked throughout the day.

Zac had helped her crawl inside, although they'd both giggled like children when she tumbled inside onto the living room floor.

"Blurrrrrrrgh," she groaned into the pillow when she finally stirred at a quarter past eleven. Her mouth tasted dry and bitter, and her head pounded from the booze. She crawled out of bed and checked the time. *Shit! Way to sleep the entire freaking day away, River, and miss lunch with Py*—

The phone rang. After clearing her throat a few times, she answered in a creaky, thick voice. "Hello?"

"Good morning, sweetie," Pythia greeted her. "Was just checking to see if everything is okay. You're an hour late for brunch."

"I'm okay, just a little tired."

Her mentor chuckled. "You sound awful."

"I feel awful," River replied.

"Go take a bath and lay down. I'll talk to you later."

"No, no, no, it's all good. I meant to call you anyway. I need to report a serious breach."

"Tell me what happened."

"My neighbor is having troubles with his ex always coming around still, right? Well, last night she pulled some new shit out of her box of tricks like I've never seen. It can't be natural."

"Some potions are more powerful than others," Pythia replied.

"No, this wasn't only a potion. Maybe in part, but something else was going on. Something sinister and dark and oily. It felt dirty, Pythia. If you saw the way he behaved when she was near, you'd know no lust potion could sway that man."

"We don't know for a fact she used dark magic."

"Then there needs to be an inquiry," River blurted out.

Silence met her, a long pause before Pythia replied. "You're demanding an inquiry, love? You're only a junior sorceress."

"Yes. I am. Something awful almost happened last night." She imagined Pythia kneading her temples. In hindsight, she wished she hadn't dumped the wine.

"All right. I'll speak with the other senior witches and pull together an investigation circle."

"Thank you."

"You owe me though."

"Whatever you want. I'm sorry for missing our brunch today."

After rescheduling for another date the next week, they ended the call, and River dragged her sorry butt into the shower. By noon, she felt human enough to bake fresh blueberry muffins. The remnants of a hangover flit at the edges of her awareness, throbbing on occasion despite aspirin and frequent sips of water while they baked. Once her bounty of sweet delights cooled, she carried the entire batch to Zac's place and knocked on the door.

He answered shirtless and clothed in only gym shorts. His television played in the background. "How'd you sleep?" he asked, covering a yawn with one palm.

"Not too bad. Did I wake you?"

"Nah, I've just been too lazy to make coffee. Guess I should do that. Want some?"

"Please."

After they filled their bellies with baked goods and sugar-laden caffeine, Zac blended up some virgin daiquiris to enjoy on the back porch. River took a seat on a cushy lounge chair and surveyed his drab share of the rear yard. The dull patches of short grass lacked any kind of ornamentation compared to the green paradise she'd cultivated on the other side of the fence. She had stepping stones, a tranquil fountain, and a birdbath often inhabited by hummingbirds during the warmer months.

And River knew he liked her setup because she'd caught him sitting out on his patio and enviously watching her feathered visitors. After that, he suddenly returned home with hummingbird feeders of his own.

"I don't know what the hell I'm doing," he admitted. "I come out here and think, 'hell yeah, I'm going to the greenhouse today,' and when I get there, some clerk tells me everything I like is high maintenance or lots of trouble to plant."

"High maintenance means they're more rewarding when they thrive," River teased, nudging him with her shoulder. "Let's try some winter vegetables and plants. Like I said before, pansies thrive over the winter. We'll buy more of those and some ornamental cabbage to border the walking path in the front."

"Ornamental... cabbage?" he echoed.

"Yup. They're really pretty. Purple, white, and pink."

"But it's cabbage."

"And they're pretty. You said you wanted it to look dazzling," she countered.

"Fine, but you have to do something with me first."

He looked too eager and suspicious to be trusted. "What?"

Zac flashed his dimpled grin. "Come to the skating rink with me."

Skeptical of his motivations, River shifted in the chair and gazed toward the back of the yard, where the wooden fence separated the duplex property from the wilderness bordering their land. The local werewolf alpha owned a couple thousand acres of it. He'd moved a few years ago to another house beyond the city limits instead. Apparently, they ran a nonprofit wolf sanctuary on the property. At least, that was their story for the public.

"Mmm. I don't skate."

"Then what's that photo of you at your place?" he asked.

River grunted. "A bad photo of me in skates."

"You were pretty young," he ventured in an encouraging tone.

And skinny, she thought bitterly, albeit for reasons that had nothing to do with her personal outlook toward weight and everything to do with the memories of her pushy father's obsession with fitness. "Okay, so maybe I used to be a member of the Texas Speed Club. A long time ago."

To his credit, Zac didn't laugh. His eyes crinkled at the corners when he smiled and he leaned over to nudge her. "Yeah, and…?"

"I was the quad skating champion for two years in a row," she mumbled.

"So why aren't you proud of it? Isn't that kind of an accomplishment?"

"I guess."

"What am I missing here?"

River sighed and stirred her drink around, mixing the pretty colors Zac had tediously layered into the frozen beverage. He must have taken bartending classes at some point in his life, or practiced way too much in his kitchen. He had a glass-fronted cabinet filled with various cordials and mixers.

"I used to love skating at first. I'd go once a weekend with my friends and hang out. We'd have fun. Then one night my dad wandered in to pick me up instead of Mom, and he saw this flyer for the local skate club. Signed me up without asking me. He *insisted.* It was his way of melting the fat off my ass and getting me in shape, so I wouldn't shame him anymore. He didn't like everybody knowing he had a fat kid at home."

Zacarias stared at her in disbelief. "What? Are you serious?"

"My dad is Ronny Jackson. Earthquake Jackson was what they called him when he played for the Cowboys."

At first, his blank stare made her exhale in relief until his eyes grew owlish and wide. Recognition dawned at last. "*He's* your father?"

Dammit. "Yeah."

"I heard he's a dick," Zac said, sounding tentative.

"He is." Nodding her head, River slouched down in the seat and sipped from the glass again. "I lost about forty pounds the first summer and won some small competitions. Then next year came, and I won the championship. Dad was real proud. I busted my ass to get there, but I just did it for him, you know?"

It was the only time her father had ever hugged her. Ever said he was proud, making all other accomplishments seem inconsequential by comparison in his eyes.

"So why'd you quit?"

"It's…" She dragged in a few measured breaths, but the pressure built in her chest anyway as she tried to blink away the burning behind her lids. "All this time and it still upsets me. You'd think I would be over it by now."

"We don't have to talk about it if you don't want to," Zac said, backpedaling. His beautiful green eyes became apologetic. "Sorry, it was a bad idea. I saw the photo on your wall and thought you had a secret love for skating."

"No," she said decisively. "Let's go." She sucked up the rest of her frozen drink and powered through the brain freeze. "Gonna find my skates."

"You know you can borrow some at the rink."

"And put my feet in other people's stank? Hell no."

A big grin spread over Zac's face. Leaving his seat, he collected their glasses and leaned down to kiss her, tropical passion fruit and mango flavoring his lips.

"How long do you need?"

"I'll meet you out front in an hour."

"An hour to get skates?" Zacarias asked with humor in his voice. He smiled again, his friendly eyes filled with warmth.

"An hour to get skates and change into acceptable clothes. And to do something with my hair."

"Are you serious? You look great."

Doubting in his sincerity, she glanced down at tight and clinging yoga pants molded to her ass and thighs. The black material didn't leave much to the imagination and revealed every curve, dimple, and wrinkle. She'd donned them after a drowsy shower along with thong sandals and a V-neck T-shirt.

"Yeah… not exactly the best skating attire. It's not that I'm shy about wearing leggings and shit, I mean, if people don't like it, they can look away, but I've heard these things split like wet tissue paper sometimes."

His grin widened even more. "I wouldn't complain."

"I bet you wouldn't. I'm not taking the risk though. Promise I'll make it quick."

Urged by impulse, River took advantage of the recent change to their friendship status and stole a brief kiss before scurrying back to her house.

I hope my skates still fit. She had no idea whether or not they were in any condition for casual skating at the rink.

Fifty pounds of junk tumbled out of the closet when she tugged open the door, a combination of clothes she could no longer fit, shoe boxes, and old books for the yard sale she always planned but never organized. Somewhere in the dark recesses of a closet filled with jeans she hadn't worn since high school, she found her roller skates beneath a pile of folded blankets.

While old, they still looked as new as they were the day her mother bought them. The outdated style contrasted the conditioned leather and clean laces, but she tried them on and wiggled her toes in the abundant space. Over the years, she'd performed occasional maintenance, kept them clean, dry, and safely stored.

They'd work.

Despite her claim of needing an hour, River made it back to Zac's place in half the time. He answered the door with a pair of rollerblades in hand

"Promise you won't laugh if I'm rusty."

Zac took his time to ponder it.

"*Promise,*" she repeated.

"Okay, okay. I promise I won't laugh if you land on your ass a few times."

River landed on her butt twice in the first hour, and as promised, he didn't laugh. He did slyly remark, while dusting off her bottom with one of his large hands, that the ample amount of natural cushioning seemed to soften the fall.

She mock-scowled at him.

The small rink in town only opened twice a week, operating Friday and Saturday nights from six to midnight. A mix of 80's and 90's music played over the sound system, and a disco ball hung in the center of the spacious room. Zac took River by the hand and led her on several circuits while she acclimated to traveling on eight wheels again.

Knowledge of how to skate flooded back to her eventually, and like riding a bike, her confidence returned when she broke loose of Zac and eased into the crowd at her own pace. She weaved in and out between slower skaters while skillfully pushing off.

Her thighs were going to kill her the next day.

And every blissful second of agony would be worth it, paired with the memory of the best date she'd ever had in her adult life. Grinning, she glanced over her shoulder to spy Zac cruising behind her, focused on either her graceful movements or her ass.

Testing her muscle memory, she reversed her stride and turned backward to keep him in view. She wobbled at first, regained balance, and gave Zac a moment to catch up.

"You look good," he said as he took both of her hands again. A warm, satisfied flush spread through River's limbs when he linked their fingers.

"So do you."

Zac's chuckle filled her with happiness. She peered into his gold-rimmed green eyes, becoming bashful when the lights dimmed and a slow R&B song drifted from the speakers. The voices of Boyz II Men crooned a song meant for lovemaking while her new boyfriend gave her a silly grin.

Then he began humming it under his breath until the second verse when he began to speak aloud, words colored by a hint of his native accent. She stared.

"Don't you dare sing to me," she hissed playfully, half hoping he'd disregard her and continue. The rest of the couples with joined hands skated in their own little worlds, oblivious to anyone else.

If he tells me he'll make love to me like I want him to, I'll combust into a ball of sexually-frustrated flames, River thought. She'd never endure long enough for him to make it to the end of the song!

Thankfully, it wasn't necessary. Willing her lady parts to cool down, she focused on the glee she experienced whenever a woman on the sidelines shot them an envious glance in passing. Every time she chastised herself for behaving like a horny teenager, her body cooperated a little more.

When the song ended, they vacated the floor for a concession stand pit stop. Zac paid for their shared nacho order before she had a chance to fish some money from her pocket.

"I can pay for my own food. But thanks," she added with a genuinely appreciative tone, mostly concerned he would, at some point, feel obligated to always step in as the provider. More than anything, River wanted to be different from Lucia, who expected wealth to be thrown at her.

"You can buy the next round," he assured her.

They claimed a small table tucked away in the corner, gaining a reprieve from the music blasting over the speakers. River dug into the cheese and meat-loaded tortillas without hesitation, too hungry to eat like a bird.

"How does it feel to be on the floor again?"

"Exhausting," she answered, following with a big smile. "And it's great. Thanks. You know, for noticing."

"You're welcome."

Once all the chips were gone, they took turns dragging their fingers through the pooled remnants of melted cheese at the bottom.

"I had a boyfriend who hated when I did this."

"It's the best part," Zac said. He snickered. "You've dated a lot of assholes."

"Hey, you can't say much."

"True. With her, it was always calorie counting. I'd offer to take her to the gym with me, or workout at home, but she was afraid she'd bulk up."

A frown creased her forehead. "Naturally having a thin body is one thing, but I'd rather bulk up than starve myself to be thin."

"Wanna hit the gym with me?"

Her gut instinct was to accept, but the little niggling voice of her father whispered in the back of her head. Nobody wanted a buff woman who looked like a man. "Maybe not," she backtracked.

"If you change your mind, I'm game. I go Monday, Tuesday, Thursday, and Friday during my lunch break."

"I do yoga at home," she offered in a lame attempt at an excuse. "I do like heavy lifting sometimes. It's fun. I tried kickboxing lessons for a little while too, but I never stuck with any of it."

"How come?"

"Dad used to say I'd get muscles like a man," she mumbled. "That's why he put me into skating. He wanted me to be thin and pretty like Mom." Who was a cheerleader on the team back then. "He meant well, but I guess…"

"Riv," Zac said as he reached across the table and took her hand. "Don't get me wrong, you were very pretty in the picture on your wall, but the you of *then* doesn't compare with the you in front of me now. You look fantastic."

She rolled her shoulders a little and avoided eye contact.

"You are amazing. I mean, I wouldn't want you to get as buff as me or anything—" He winked before continuing. "—but only 'cause I'd feel threatened, like I'm slacking off. Come on. There's a retired marine at the gym who does kickboxing lessons. Come sign up. I'll add you to my membership if you don't already have one."

Man, screw Dad. I can do what I want. "I'll come with you and give it a try."

"Just once, and if you don't love it anymore, you don't have to come back."

She sipped her cherry-lemonade slush and considered it. "Deal."

After all, if she had the confidence to face petty witches like Lucia, hitting the machines at the gym would be a cakewalk.

***

Thanks to a night of skating and throwing caution to the wind, River could barely crawl out of bed the next day. Zac laughed at her over the phone and showed up with a package of Oreos. They shared them in front of a movie and took it easy while River waited for any news from Pythia regarding her investigation request.

Witch's inquiries were big deals in the covens, requiring a circle of seven to investigate claims of wrongdoing. Depending on the severity of the crime, punishments ranged from imprisonment to temporary or permanent power binding.

Or even execution in the most extreme cases.

Maybe it was a blessing in disguise because it took her two more days to recover from their impromptu skate session. On the third day of her recovery, as she lay sprawled face down on the couch watching Netflix, her best and longest friend phoned her over Skype.

"Hey, chica. How's it going?"

"It's going slowly," River complained. "You're interrupting my Netflix binge."

"Sorry. Why do you look like crap?"

"I went outside into the terrifying world, and this thing called exercise kicked my ass."

Marcy laughed. "Wow. That's sad, Riv."

"I know, but it was worth it. Zac took me skating, but now my legs don't want to cooperate and everything from sitting on the couch to walking upstairs hurts."

Her friend's face brightened. "Wait, you mean to tell me you finally went out on a date with your smokin' neighbor?"

"Yes."

"Awesome, then you need to come down here to visit me. And bring him too. The resort would be an amazing getaway for both of you."

"Hey, it's not that kind of relationship yet, and I can't afford that kind of thing right now."

"What is there to afford? I'm offering you a free, all-expenses-paid trip to our island."

Zac's characteristic knock thudded against the front door. She peered out the window and saw him idling on the stoop and examining her flowers.

"Just a sec, Marcy. He's at the door."

"Oooh, I wanna see."

Groaning, River abandoned her comfy sprawl and answered the door. Zac leaned in and claimed a quick kiss the moment the door opened. "Afternoon, sunshine. You been hiding away in here working?"

"Yes and no. I've been recovering."

His deep, warm chuckle sent a pleasant chill running down her spine. "I thought as much, so I came bearing gifts. A massage after we get back from the gym."

"Take it, girl! Take it!"

Zac's gaze snapped around toward Marcy's voice, and his brows raised high. From the angle provided at her front door, he couldn't see into her living room. "Shit. Sorry, I didn't realize you had a guest."

"Sorta. Can you give me a couple minutes? I'm chatting with a friend online."

"Sure. I can wait next door if you'd like."

"Nah, come in and say hello."

Against her better judgment, River dragged Zacarias in front of the computer and pulled up a chair.

"Whoa, okay, I agree with your assessment. He is a hottie." Marcy's cheerful face filled the monitor, and it was obvious she was giving Zac a look over.

"This is my neighbor, Zacarias."

Zac cleared his throat.

"And boyfriend," she added.

"So you're the orchid-rescuing photographer. Nice to meet you," Zac greeted.

"Ah, so she's spoken about me but told me almost nothing about you." Marcy sighed and shook her head. "River, what am I going to do with you?"

"I was getting to it, sheesh. You're halfway across the world, and there's lots to catch up on," she grumbled, much to Zac's amusement.

"Don't listen to her," Marcy said. "She moved away first. Now she's sore I live in another country. All she has to do is accept my husband's kindness and fly here to visit both of us."

"I don't know, Marcy. It's expensive," River said. "Way too much money to pay for me to make a random visit."

"What if I pay and we make it a vacation together?" Zac offered.

River whirled around and stared at him, jaw dropping. "Absolutely *not*."

"Why can't I?"

"Because… because you can't, that's why."

"Honestly, you two. Look, Teo owns the island. The whole point of what I'm sayin' is that neither of you has to pay anything. Flying you down this way is chump change as far as he's concerned. If it makes you feel better, consider it a few years' worth of birthdays owed."

"See, it's a gift, River," Zac said as he joined Marcy's side of the argument. "And my mother always taught me to never turn down a gift. It's rude."

Then Marcy and Zac began chatting at one another in Spanish, too fast for her to understand, while gesturing toward River.

"Hey!" she shouted.

The conversation continued for a moment longer, and she grew increasingly horrified at their behavior. What the hell were they saying about her? Why were they laughing?

"What?" Marcy asked. "We were only talking."

"Or possibly plotting behind your back," Zac said. They both snickered.

"I didn't even know you could speak Spanish too," River muttered. "Anyway, it's rude to tune out your English-only speaking pal. Good grief, couldn't you two wait to meet in person before ganging up on me?"

"Love you, chica. Chloe is coming to visit us at Christmas, by the way. She asked about you recently. Now I'll finally have good news to share with her. Talk to you soon."

"Love you too." After ending the call, River sighed and turned around to face Zacarias. As she scowled at his smug grin, and those incredible dimples, she rose from the seat and stalked past him on the way to change for their gym date.

"You're welcome," he said when she returned dressed down in a tank and loose sweats.

"You're such a jerk."

"A lovable jerk, I hope." His green eyes shone with amusement.

"The best jerk," she relented.

Her opinion of him changed an hour later. He'd taken off the afternoon from work in honor of their first visit as a couple to the gym. Grudgingly, River allowed him to add her to his membership and accepted an oval-shaped plastic tag with a barcode printed on one side. She attached it to her key ring.

Zac showed a small measure of mercy and started her off on the treadmill for a warm-up walk. She watched with envy as he went from a brisk walk to loping like a gazelle within minutes, all the while feeling like the sloppy pity date when a sporty blonde moved onto the machine on his other side. She checked him out, and to his credit, he remained oblivious.

Or pretended to be oblivious. She dropped her rag and bent over, her bottom in clear view of him, and all Zac did was hit stop on his machine and patiently wipe it down while suggesting, very loudly to me, that we should hit the weight room together.

"Where should I start?"

"Where would you like to be stronger?" he asked.

She considered the question and peeked down at her thighs. In the aftermath of their night out at the rink, she'd hated how sore and tight she felt. "My legs."

He set her up on a machine and let her pick the weight setting. With his instructions, she settled into the seat with her feet resting on the bars. River squeezed with her knees and closed her thighs to lift the weight, feeling awkward and exposed with each release.

"This feels indecent," she muttered up at him.

Zac grinned. "I didn't design the machine." He hung around for the first set.

Exasperated, River paused after a rep and glanced up at him. "What's the look for?"

"Just thinking a little. That's all."

"Thinking about what?" She stopped, thighs burning, and slouched down in the seat with her eyes closed and sweat trickling down her brow. She wiped her forehead with a cloth.

"Thinking you shouldn't cheat yourself," Zac replied. He leaned over and added twenty pounds, then wandered off to the next machine.

For a moment, she wished she could make him go up in flames, glaring at his back. Luckily for him, such powers were beyond her ability without her enchanted pyro band—and she'd left all of her magical jewelry in the car.

"You asshole," she muttered instead.

Though he stood with his back to her, the angle of his head provided enough hint to see the corner of his mouth rise. In a childish fit, she hurled her towel at his head. Then she grunted through the remaining set.

While the additional weight had been difficult, it wasn't beyond her ability. Upon completing her workout, she rose and stretched out her hamstrings until the heat faded.

A stroke of inspiration and the joy of payback led her to return his earlier favor and add more weight to the arm curl he'd occupied. His biceps strained in the most wondrous way imaginable.

Impressive? He was only a couple shy of raising the entire thing.

No matter the activity she and Zac did together, they had a great, albeit teasing and playful, time. With him, there was no judgment or bitching, only fun in its simplest form. He didn't try to wow her with sparkly gifts or fancy dinners at stuffy restaurants.

Deep down, she had to wonder if it was all too good to be true.

CHAPTER 6

A week after River first asked for assistance, Pythia appeared on her porch to deliver a message in person.

"I wanted to let you know the local circle has come to a decision."

"Oh?" River had just finished ironing her hair, straightening every curl over the tedious course of four hours from start to finish. She'd been anxious for a change, something new for her evening date with Zac.

"Yes. The Trinity has decided there's some merit to your accusations, and I thought you'd find one tidbit interesting. Your immoral friend isn't actually in the records book," Pythia said.

"What? Aren't all witches?"

"All known witches. Some witches develop the gift without knowing their ancestry or receiving training. You were fortunate, River. Your mother raised you in our world, and you've always known you were different. Imagine if you were adopted and raised by strangers."

River sighed. "I guess. Maybe that's why her attitude about what she did to Zac sucks. I just can't imagine anyone raised in the community would want to steal another person's free will."

"Agreed."

"Still, she's damn well-trained for someone not raised in the know."

Pythia shrugged. "I've seen it before. Young women, and sometimes the occasional man, find themselves in a situation where the power emerges. Sometimes it's defensive, other times it's while studying mysticism and the occult. Regardless of how it's happened, we'll pay a visit to Lucia Aguilar this evening."

"Can I come?"

While considering the request, Pythia crossed her arms and regarded her for a long moment of quiet study before responding. "You can observe, but only that. You don't want anyone saying you tainted the evidence."

River crossed her fingers over her heart. "I'll keep my hands in my pockets the entire time."

"Good. Come with me then. I'm on my way now, but I wanted to stop by to let you know."

River glanced at the adjacent driveway. Zacarias hadn't returned yet, and he'd texted to warn her of a possible late day in the office. She grabbed her purse from the table by the door and hurried outside to join Pythia in the older witch's truck.

The forty-five-minute drive took them into the wealthy, suburban neighborhoods of San Antonio. They pulled into the parking lot of an affluent condominium with overpriced apartment rentals to find the other witches awaiting their arrival beside a glossy silver Bentley. Grace, the oldest of the ladies, always drove in style.

"It's about time you arrived, Pythia. Honestly, lead by example and show a little responsibility to your junior sorceress," the youngest of the six witches teased, voice lighthearted and smile radiant despite her words.

Pythia rolled her eyes. "Of course, Claudia. In the future, I'll aspire to be like you and fly twice the speeding limit."

Claudia beamed. "What the police don't see won't hurt them. Remember that a well-placed misdirection jinx is always your friend when driving."

Although River had known most of the women since puberty, when her powers first emerged and her mother began dragging her to coven brunches and get-togethers, she hung back as a silent observer. These were witches older and more powerful than her who had seen several lifetimes. And for some reason, many of them had taken an unusual interest in her as a child, always giving her gifts and encouraging her magic.

"So, this is your protege." A woman with steel-hued hair stepped forward and appraised River with a critical eye. "Don't be shy, child. Come, come. A pleasure to finally meet you, young lady. I'm Rhona, formerly from the Daughters of the Sun on the West Coast. I've recently moved here to fill a vacant spot on the inner circle."

Still shy, River nodded in greeting and cleared her throat. "River Jackson."

"Yes, of course. We were all quite jealous Pythia would be the one to mentor you when—" A second witch elbowed Rhona, interrupting her. "Erm, anyway, it's a pleasure."

"I know your mother," another witch said as she swooped in and took River by the hands. "Cynthia was right, you've become such a lovely young woman. Do you remember me?"

"Um, not really…."

"I'm Daphne. I gave you a silver mortar and pestle when you were just a little girl. You told me you wanted to become the best alchemist in the world."

Heat surged to River's cheeks since she only felt like a mediocre alchemist with no extraordinary ability. "Thank you. I still use that one," she mumbled.

Grace placed a slim pair of spectacles on her face. "Well then, ladies, let's not overwhelm her with introductions and chatter. We are here to discuss an unregistered witch, yes? Then let's do that. Come along, dear, these old bones are tired and I'd like to be home in my bed by nine."

"Agreed," Rhona said.

With a purposeful stride, Grace started toward the main doors of the condo after taking River by the hand. The other six fell into line behind her. "Now, please, tell us how you discovered this witch."

"Well, I was out for a stroll in my feline form when my neighbor brought me inside his house… and I was trapped," River explained. Fibbing when necessary, she cleared her throat. "Anyway, I was there when she poured something in his drink. I knocked it off the table."

"As cats often do," Rhona said.

"Right. Um, so she kept trying to do it. Really pushy methods of trying to drug him with this lust potion."

"While we don't approve of such potions, there's no law against them." Rhona pursed her lips.

"I know. That's why I took matters into my own hands. Pythia helped me brew a curative."

"You brewed an antidote to a lust potion?"

River nodded and pressed the elevator call button in the lobby. "Well, more like a preventative potion. I figured, if I could keep him from being affected, maybe she'd give up and leave him alone."

"I take it that wasn't the case," Daphne said.

They all spilled inside the same elevator without separating. The lobby itself had screamed wealth and sophistication with pricey portraits on the walls, tan leather furnishings over glossy marble floors, and dangling chandelier fixtures.

How much does she spend a month living here? It can't be less than a few grand.

"Yeah. She only became more desperate, and since he's a nice guy, he'd tolerate her a few minutes then shoo her off because she always came with some legitimate excuse. A week ago, when she arrived, something was different. I felt the power pulsing around her like some kind of miasma. My potions had no effect. Zacarias was like... I dunno. He was clearly ensorcelled."

Grace studied her curiously. "What did you do?"

"I, uh, got him away from his house first. When that didn't work out exactly, I..."

"You what?"

An uncomfortable prickle crawled up her nape. "I kissed him."

While Pythia had already listened to her retelling of the events, the other women gazed upon River with varying degrees of shock and disbelief on their aged faces.

"My dear, are you claiming to have broken a compulsion with a kiss?" Grace asked.

"Well… I'm not claiming anything. I really don't know. But after that, he was clearheaded enough to kick her out of his house. That's when she confronted me. She accused *me* of bewitching him."

Pythia and Rhona nodded at one another, appearing to communicate in an eerie, nonverbal way. The latter cleared her throat. "Well then, let's proceed as planned."

The elevator doors opened into a carpeted hallway. Pythia took the lead and moved to the last unit with the seven other witches trailing behind her in a single-file line and River at the rear. She'd never spectated an investigation by the circle before, only heard of them and the unfavorable outcomes when a witch was found guilty of negligence.

Rarely did the anonymous Mystic Trinity—the maiden, mother, and crone—choose anything less than imprisonment or death once the court of seven passed judgment. Why their identities remained secret was anyone's guess, though River suspected it had to do with diminishing the number of frivolous requests for their time they'd receive. Instead, they guided their peers from the shadows.

Upon reaching a door at the end of the hall, Grace and Pythia stepped forward first. The former knocked, and all others fell into line, paying her some measure of respect.

The door opened to frame the slender, leggy model in a black, spaghetti strap summer dress. She tossed her scarlet hair over one shoulder and appraised their group. "What do *you* want?" she asked River.

Grace moved to the forefront. "Lucia Aguilar, you stand accused of performing an act of black witchcraft. We are aware of your gift and have come to make a formal review."

"And who the hell are you to barge in on my home like this?"

Rhona fixed Lucia with a stern glare. "We are the circle of the craft, young lady, and you'd do well to show us some respect. If you know enough to brew potions, you certainly know who we are."

Lucia's mouth twisted as if she'd tasted something sour. "Even if you are an old biddy council of witches, what gives you the right to barge into my personal home—"

In the next moment, before River could warn the accused witch to behave, Grace casually flicked two fingers through the air. The rings decorating them glowed bright purple and blue, an ominous precursor of what was to come.

Tried to warn her, River thought.

A magic gust thrust Lucia into her home, and the next sweep of Grace's liver-spotted hand slid Lucia out of their way. Magic firmly placed her beside the luxury kitchen's long counter, and no matter how much she strained to move, all she managed to budge was her head. The tendons of her neck stood out, and her jaw tightened from the effort until at last, she abandoned the attempt.

"Now, now. If you're going to be a spoiled, disrespectful brat, dearie, this is where you'll remain while we conduct our search."

"You have no authority to be here."

Pythia smiled and closed the door behind them once River stepped inside. "On the contrary, my dear, the Daughters of the Moon hold complete autonomy in this part of the country when it comes to magical matters. Be a peach and stop fighting. Things will go much smoother if you cooperate."

Lucia glowered from where the witch elder bound her.

Good. Not so nice when someone takes away your control, now is it?

River couldn't help but feel smug while observing the proceedings. The women fanned out through the expensive apartment, reminding her of a squad of arcane police detectives, each one armed with a crystal dangling from a black cord. Some sparkled, others glowed, and one twirled around in circles while emitting buzzing noises. Fascinated, she remained out of their way.

"We'll check the upstairs," one witch said. She and another elder moved up the metal steps to the upper level. Sophisticated crisscrossing designs decorated the black railing and revealed hints of the room beyond it.

"River, see how the crystal is leaning?" Pythia called, drawing River over. The quartz point tugged against the cord. "It means there's something emitting power this way. Open that closet for me, dear."

The accordion-style, slatted doors opened without a squeak, revealing a space meant for a washer and dryer. Instead of machines, Lucia had set up a brewing station. Glass jars filled with various herbs and potions lined the upper shelf in a haphazard manner, and three high-end slow cookers sat on the wooden table set into the narrow space.

Pythia clicked her tongue. "What do we have here, hmm?" She leaned down and sniffed the thin line of steam rising from the first cooker. "Jasmine, vanilla, and a touch of mandrake if I'm not mistaken. Brewing up love potions, I see."

"I use them in my work and at the agency. They don't hurt anyone."

"Your technique is crude but effective." Pythia unplugged the pot and Lucia made a low sound that sounded close to a snarl. "While love potions are a gray area, we advise all young witches to stay away from them."

"I am hardly a child. Do not treat me as one."

Pythia glanced to her left. "Rhona, are you able to determine the identity of this one's past life?"

Rhona shook her head. "She must be a newly born witch. Fresh to the cycle."

"Ah. I suspected as much when I couldn't recognize her."

Interest piqued, River's gaze darted from witch to witch, studying their expressions when the others came to the same consensus.

Unlike wizards who lived indefinitely within one body as white-haired sages, witches returned to life one generation after the next, and the most powerful of them reincarnated shortly after death in a new infant body. The weakest sometimes fizzled out like celestial bodies in the cosmos, never to be seen again.

According to her mother and Pythia, River had never completed a previous lifetime before. River had also never met another young, new witch like herself either since most witches chose to remain childless. It made her pity the situation all the more.

It would have been nice to have a friend like me. Since her birth and induction into their world, she'd been treated differently, coddled by her mother and friends. Was that why? Because they were afraid she'd make some grievous, awful mistake?

After neutralizing the potion with a few deft pours of some ingredients and essential oils on the shelves, Grace donned a pair of kitchen mitts and removed the pot to the bathroom sink. She poured it out.

Pythia put her crystal away then cleared her throat. "Only an experienced alchemist can determine the potency of her brews, and it's easy to cross the line and push a man, or a woman, into reckless infatuation. I had a friend once many years ago who didn't heed my warning. She awakened to her young suitor standing above her bed. He'd broken in during the dead of night, and because he'd seen her smiling at the baker that morning, decided she no longer loved only him. He cut her throat so no one else could ever have her."

Maybe the story wasn't anything new to River since she'd heard it before as their best and most frightening cautionary tale, but she rubbed her throat anyway.

"She survived of course, but just barely. So, at any rate, my dear, you'll want to leave this alone. In fact, I do insist you attend studies with Georgina before you attempt any further potion making endeavors. You're lucky you haven't poisoned yourself, storing everything this way."

River winced. Georgina wasn't an elder, but she was the next closest thing and a stern taskmaster who didn't believe in leniency. She had taught River how to make her first potions but only after months of scrubbing pots, drying herbs, and memorizing trait lists for over a hundred ingredients.

"I don't—" A stern look from Rhona made Lucia stop and clear her throat. "Fine."

"Excellent," Rhona said as she placed a card on the counter with the contact information of a dozen witches. "I'll inform Georgina to expect your call within the week. Until then, no potions."

Two of the elders started clearing the shelves, confiscating Lucia's ingredients and tools.

"Nothing worrisome upstairs," Daphne reported. "A few books and charms. Most of them were fiction on Wicca with inaccurate assumptions regarding our practice." She paused before adding, "A couple were decent, I'll give her that."

"Then you should all be leaving now. As you can see, there is nothing here." Lucia raised her chin and stared the group down. "Only a jealous cow."

"Jealous cow?" Maybe River didn't get paid to prance up and down a runway in her underwear, but she had nothing to be jealous about. Her temper flared, but before she could speak again, Pythia placed a hand on her shoulder.

"There is *also* the matter of your unregistered state," Pythia said. "Considering your... ignorance of our community and rules, no formal action will be taken against you. However, we will document you in our records for spontaneous audits."

"Audits?"

"Yes. We review the actions of all our kind from time to time to ensure rules are being followed, as well as to offer guidance and assistance where needed."

Lucia's scowl deepened, forming creases between the corner of her mouth and nose. River expected her to get them Botox'ed soon. "I haven't done anything wrong."

"And you won't. If you do, we will return, and it won't be to play nice. Our society has survived centuries for a reason, and a stray witch will not ruin it for the many," Grace said.

"I haven't ruined anything. All of this over one petty witch wanting my man?"

"Your man?" River spat out. "All of this is because he doesn't want you and you tried to force it!"

"River," Pythia said in a gentle voice.

With the patience of a saint, Grace carried on despite the interruption. "You'll be expected to allow any elder of our circle entry whenever we return. If you have any questions, you're welcome to call the number on that card given to you."

"Get out," Lucia spat. "There's nothing here, so you need to leave."

They filed out of the apartment and left the smoldering, bratty model behind. River forced steel into her backbone and refused to look over her shoulder, quiet until they reached the elevator.

"I don't like her," Rhona grumped once they were on the way down.

"Nothing but meanness and disrespect in that one," Daphne agreed.

"Unfortunately, we can't do anything because she's a foul-tempered bitch," Grace said, shrugging. "I'll drop by in a few days, make sure she isn't up to more potion mischief."

"If she doesn't call Georgina, can you *make* her take lessons?" River asked.

The elevator dinged, allowing them to step inside.

"Yes. Otherwise it's a hazard, a potential to cause large-scale harm. Tell me, my dear, what happens if you substitute coriander instead of cilantro in a detoxification cordial?" she asked River.

"What? Well, that depends, I guess. In America, we refer to the plant as cilantro and the seeds as coriander. It's different in the UK. They merely call the entire plant coriander there, so you wouldn't be substituting anything at all. If you're speaking of coriander seeds, that would increase the potency and strip the body of all its beneficial bacteria too."

Pythia grinned while the witches around her raised their brows and nodded in approval.

"Very impressive," Rhona murmured. "Most witches fall for Grace's trick questions, especially young ones."

"Georgina's a great teacher," River said.

Pythia nodded in agreement. "She is one of the best. And now you see how easily one may make a harmless, careless mistake without realizing? She could have caused irreversible harm to your handsome friend if she'd used the wrong ingredient."

"So what would happen if Lucia refused to go?"

"We would bind her powers, of course. One as young as she would have no choice or protection against it. We can't very well force everyone to join the circle, but we *can* require them to undergo the necessary training to be on their own."

A cold chill trickled down her spine. River couldn't begin to imagine having her powers taken away from her. It would be like losing a part of herself.

The elevator reached the ground level and let them off. The witches filed outside to their vehicles, which faded into view once they came close enough.

Grace removed a single leaf from beneath the windshield wiper of her car, and the misdirection veil lifted from the area. "We may not have discovered any proof of demonic fraternization, but you've done a good thing this day, River. Georgina will set her straight."

Rhona hugged her in parting, and the other witches gave her reassuring smiles before the group dispersed, each to her individual automobile.

Once they settled in Pythia's truck, River dragged her hands through her hair. "I was positive…" She buckled in and sighed before sinking back against the lavender-scented seats.

"Nothing outright forbidden, no," Pythia replied. She pressed her lips together in a thin line and stared out the window at Lucia's building without starting the truck. "Quite the temper on her though."

River snorted. "She destroyed my front garden like a child throwing a tantrum."

"Best avoid her if you can. But if she continues to make trouble, let me know."

"Sure."

"I mean it, River. You didn't endear yourself to her at all today, and I expect you to report any retaliation she might attempt."

"I promise, Pythia."

"Good. How do you feel about stopping at Taco Bell on the way home?"

"Like I'm not in the mood to wreck my stomach. I actually have a date in two hours."

"Then we better get you back on time and unbloated."

CHAPTER 7

Zacarias sat outside of River's house in his Jag, waiting for her to emerge for their date. Two weeks of seeing her drove him up the wall with inner turmoil. In some ways, spending time alone with River was his own personal hell; he was a thirsty man in a desert, with a glass of water always beyond reach.

Was it too early to share his secret? Years ago, he'd trusted Lucia and told her about the werejaguars of his native country. When he filed for divorce, telling the world about his kind was the first threat to pass her lips. She even threatened to go to a newspaper until Zac's friend Harrison called a giant dragon shifter from Hollywood. He appeared one afternoon in their living room in the heat of the dispute and told Lucia she wouldn't be the first human he'd devoured. Saul ended his threat by declaring he had enough money to make her parents forget they had birthed her. Before he vanished, he'd stared at her with his glowing, golden eyes and said she should know better.

Later, Zac had wondered what the dragon meant, but Harrison shrugged in an equally clueless way. "Beats me, man. But he was pretty pissed, and I'm not calling him back here to ask questions."

Almost two years passed without hearing from Lucia, even when he tried to sell the house. Now suddenly she wanted in his life again, though thankfully he hadn't seen her since the night they almost fell into bed again.

All along, he'd known he couldn't trust her, but his personal philosophy included releasing bad energy and letting go of bad blood whenever possible. Still, even he had a limit on how much forgiveness he could feel toward Lucia.

So what the hell had happened that night? Why did he almost sleep with her again? The question had boggled him ever since, despite River's pleasant company.

He hadn't even considered having another relationship until the sweet artist next door charmed her way into his life.

The phone in the beverage holder beeped at him. Zac plucked it up and glanced at his recent messages to find an apology from River.

River: Running behind. Had random crap to do this afternoon. Promise I'll be out in fifteen.
Zacarias: No problem. Take your time, sweetheart. I'll be right here.

It rang before he set it down again, flashing the name of the best friend he'd made since moving to San Antonio—or one of his best friends at least. Harrison and Thomas evenly tied and were as close to him as brothers.

"Sup, dude?" Zac answered.

"Hey, man. You free tonight? Harrison, the guys, and I were planning a trip into San Antonio."

"Strip club?"

Thomas's voice brightened. "Yeah. We've been checking out a new place each month, and Bobby has the pick this time."

"Sounds fun, but I'm gonna have to pass."

"For real? Bro, when do you ever take the time to hang out?"

"Sorry. I would, but I have a date."

"A date?"

"Yeah, you know, that fun thing you do when you take out a girl you like. Don't you take your wives out for dates anymore?"

Thomas grunted. "I know what a date is, asshole. And yes, I took Em out for dinner just a few days ago and took Ceres camping the week before that. What I *didn't* know is that you were back on the market. Who is it?"

"My neighbor, River."

"Really?"

"Yeah. So you guys have fun, and I'll catch the next one. Just maybe try to plan it a little ahead of time and not an hour before."

"What the hell happened to your spontaneity?"

"It grew up and got a job with office hours."

"Whatever, loser. Have fun on your date. We're gonna paintball this weekend."

"Harrison told me. I'll be there."

"Awesome. See you then."

He ended the call as River slipped into the passenger seat, a pretty vision in fall colors. The gold, orange, and red shades suited her mahogany skin tone, and she wore her hair ironed straight in a chestnut cascade to the small of her back.

It disappointed him a little. He preferred the original River, but couldn't deny she was amazing whether her tresses were worn curly or ironed long.

If such a thing as fated mates existed, Riv had to be the real deal. He'd never felt so strongly about a woman in all his life, the draw between them stronger than ever with each passing day.

"Where we heading?" River asked. "You never said."

"I made reservations in New Braunfels. I wanted to treat you to a nice dinner out."

"You didn't have to do that."

"I know, but I wanted to."

They spent the short drive listening to music and chatting about River's plans for his yard. She promised not to break his bank account and to teach him herself how to care for everything. Zac looked forward to the lessons because it meant spending more time with her.

Less than an hour later, they were sipping wine and sharing bacon-wrapped scallops in an intimate booth lit by candlelight.

"Where'd you find this place?"

"A friend." Zac laughed and nudged the appetizer plate with the last scallop toward her. "He brings his lady friends here and says the steaks are amazing." Though he sometimes had his suspicions about Harrison's taste in food. Raven shifters weren't known for their discerning palates and could eat anything.

"Better than yours?"

"I aim to find out."

They both ordered the steaks, and with a little friendly encouragement, he convinced River to add a lobster tail to her order.

"How come I never see you throwing any parties or anything?" she asked. "You have that huge grill for barbecues."

He considered the question and shrugged. "I dunno. I guess I like the quiet and having a place to escape without people dropping by all the time. Or, I did. Sometimes it's too quiet, you know what I mean?"

River reached across the table and set her palm over his hand. "I never realized you were lonely over there, Zac. I mean, you know what I do all day. You can knock on my door *any* time."

"I'm not lonely per se, it'd just be nice to be in good company more often. Besides, I don't want to be a distraction. You may be home, but you still work. You're running a company of your own over there, and that's hard work."

"You're not a distraction. *She* told you something like this before, didn't she?"

Even without a name, Zac knew who River was referring to. He said nothing.

"Was your ex always such a bitch?" she asked, pressing.

Was she? "I dunno. I used to tell myself that the money was to blame for our problems. We never had a lot of it when we first got together. I worked as a video game programmer for a friend's company, and she was a struggling model. Making two hundred dollars for a shoot was the highlight of her career. Hell, we didn't even see each other much the first year we were married because she was always flying off to model lingerie." He paused and glanced at River. "Is this boring you yet?"

"Why would you say that?" Her golden brown eyes were large and round. "Do I look bored?"

"No."

"Then talk. Obviously, you haven't talked to anyone about it, and I have open ears." She smiled. "So was that when everything got really shitty?"

"Kinda. She was always a little distant when she came back from a shoot. Her agent had these demands. When I left Harrison's family company to start one of my own at home, she was furious. She said we couldn't afford it and I would be living on her hard work and sweat."

River burst out laughing, a beautiful sound with genuine warmth. It encouraged him to laugh too. "She must have felt like a fool when your first game launched."

"Oh yeah. Which happened long after the crowdfunding campaign, and even longer after I found out she was screwing both her photographer and agent. We had divorced already, and I was done with women. I threw all my time into my work, so depressed I never left the house. Picked up twenty pounds. Friends had to come and drag me out for breaks."

River's amusement dwindled, and the laughter died. "It's her loss, Zacarias. You're a great guy. You help anyone in need and never ask for anything in return. And if she was too dumb to see that, then I can only say it's her loss and my gain."

He swallowed the tension in his throat and forced down the dry lump formed by his eagerness. Being around River in close quarters was always a struggle for his animal side, but he didn't want to rush things just because the jaguar inside him had chosen a mate.

The last thing Zacarias wanted was for the girl to feel like his only goal was to get physical with her. It wasn't. Even though he thought about it a *lot*, the sexual attraction wasn't what he valued most about their time together.

He loved talking to her and knowing she cared about the words leaving his mouth.

"So why were *you* single?" he asked, redirecting the focus off himself. "Weren't you dating someone when I first moved in?"

"Uh, I was, yeah. We broke up a couple weeks after you mowed the lawn the first time."

"Huh?"

"He thought you were banging me," she said with amusement glittering in her golden-brown eyes.

"That's ridiculous."

"Incredibly." She shook her head and leaned back to watch him. "I think it was for the best anyway. He was sort of controlling. We'd been fighting off and on for a while, but that was the final straw." She smiled again. "Anyway, I'm glad it ended, or we wouldn't have this chance now, right?"

"Right."

They enjoyed after-dinner coffees and shared a slice of cheesecake slathered in salted caramel. For once, River didn't argue with him regarding the check. He helped her into her coat at the door check and offered his hand.

"Walk with me for a bit?" he asked.

"All right."

There was something natural and easy about taking River's hand in his and twining their fingers. As if they'd done it a thousand times before.

"It's beautiful out tonight," River commented. She had her face tilted up to look at the stars and the moon hanging overhead.

Zac leaned down and kissed her, succumbing to the temptation that had hounded him all night. She still tasted like wine and cheesecake.

"Mm, what was that for?" she asked when his lips traveled to her ear and traced the dull throb of her pulse.

"No real reason. You look beautiful tonight, and I'm just glad we got the chance to do this."

Her radiant smile inspired him to lean down for a second, sharing a sweeter kiss without the same intensity. Then he slipped his arm around her waist and continued guiding her down the path.

"Any big plans for the weekend?" she asked.

"Paintball with the guys. You?"

"Not much. I'll probably do some art for fun and laze around in my jammies the entire time. You're welcome to join me after you get done shooting your buddies and becoming a Picasso."

"How can I turn that down?"

Time slipped away while they meandered around the park, pausing once to sit on the riverbank and watch the stars overhead like children. River's knowledge of the constellations had both surprised and impressed him. She pointed out each one and shared the old Greek myths attached to several.

Eventually, once his head was clear of the wine, Zac led the way back to the car. A quiet, companionable hush fell over them during the drive home with River's hand resting on his knee. Her touch lingered long after they pulled into the driveway, all the while they gazed at one another in silence instead of ending the night.

With intentions to end the night innocently, he kissed her tenderly at first, resting one hand on her bare shoulder. Her halter-style dress tied at her nape, the neckline plunging between her pert breasts. His hand lowered, cupping one, and then he squeezed the plump mound as she arched into his touch and moaned into his mouth, begging him with her body to continue.

River leaned away first and popped her seat belt. "Thanks for taking me out. I had a good time tonight."

"Yeah... me too." He followed her to the porch, too lovestruck to watch her from the car, even if he did live only a few yards away. She laughed at him and unlocked the door.

"I can get inside on my own, silly."

"I know. Can a man not enjoy a few minutes more of his woman's company? Damn."

River's smiles always lit her face with the natural glow and warmth of genuine compassion. Kindness. The kind of benevolence she claimed to see in him. "You can have more than a few minutes…"

He knew what she was implying. More than a few minutes. More like a night. Hours beside and beneath her. Above her, learning those full curves and soft skin. Barely restrained and desperate to be released, his inner beast roared for him to make an undeniable vow of devotion. To keep her forever in a shifters' bond.

No. Can't. She doesn't know what I am.

But he knew what he needed. Surrendering to the passion driving him, Zac seized River by a handful of her silky hair and claimed her mouth. Her natural, intoxicating scent filled his nostrils and made his blood pulse with mounting desire. Something unrecognizable lingered in her smell, and every instinct demanded for him to take her inside.

He released her instead. He didn't trust himself not to mark and bond with her before she even knew what the hell he was.

"I'll see you tomorrow, Riv."

And in the meantime, he had an appointment with a cold shower and his right hand.

"Zac, wait." The touch of her hand on his wrist stopped him midturn. He looked back at her, nostrils flaring, his tightly wound control ready to snap. "Come in with me."

***

Zac didn't give her a chance to complete the offer. Instead, he pushed through the door and swept her inside with him. He kicked it shut behind them, and then her back met the wall. His mouth slanted over hers in a thorough, exploring kiss, nipping her lower lip before he traveled lower and dipped to the neckline of her dress. River ran her fingers through his dark hair and uttered a silent prayer.

He exhaled deeply through his nostrils, breathing her in until his lips found one of her nipples. He teased the sensitive bud through the thin cotton with the edge of his teeth, nipping then soothing with his tongue. His hand slipped beneath her dress hem. "Take it off."

River didn't wait to be asked twice. She shrugged out of her coat first, and then a single clasp behind her neck and a hidden zipper on the side freed her from the dress. It pooled around her ankles, leaving her in nothing more than her panties, thigh high nylons, and kitten heels.

"God, you're beautiful."

Zac hefted her up in his arms and carried her upstairs without a grunt of exertion. Muscles rippled beneath her hands, the display of strength making her shudder and clench as electric zips raced up and down her spine.

She'd always known he was strong, but she hadn't realized he was *that* strong to lift her around like a sack of potatoes instead of a woman two small digits from two hundred pounds. Their trip to the gym should have been the first clue.

Before she could utter a word or apologize for the untidied state of her bedroom, he tossed her on the bed and turned on the light. The ceiling fixture bathed the room in fluorescent light, giving her no opportunity to hide.

Not that she'd dream of making love to Zacarias in the dark. No. She needed to see him as much as he'd wanted to see her. He removed his collared shirt first, then hitched his thumbs into the band of his boxer briefs. She only saw a hint of them, a touch of blue above his slacks, and then everything below his waist dropped to his feet. Every inch of Zac's lithe, bronzed physique was displayed for her appreciation, chiseled from broad shoulders to toned calves. Her eyes followed the dark treasure trail from his navel.

A tiny squeak of surprise left her when she took in the whole picture, and a cocky grin spread across his face. Any man with a piece as big as his had the right to grin with absolute confidence.

"Condom?" she breathed out.

"Got one."

He fetched one from his wallet and ripped the foil square with his teeth. From that moment, she surrendered to him without a second of hesitation, her decision rewarded when Zac started at her toes and kissed his way up her body, torturing her with the slow ascent. She squirmed and trembled until he settled his weight upon her—until the questing finger he slid into her warmth only worsened the cruel ache between her thighs.

River jolted and bucked her hips, craving more but unable to claim it for as long as he was above her. "Not enough," she moaned. "I need... I want..."

"Need or want?" he teased. A second finger slipped inside her, and what little control she had vanished, shattered by her impatient desire. Her hips pushed upward in a futile effort to encourage him, but Zacarias took his sweet time.

"Need!" she finally cried out.

He leaned back to gaze down at her. The lust smoldering in his eyes made her feel silly for ever doubting he could find her attractive. He loved what he saw.

As if to affirm her thoughts, his mouth lowered to one breast. His tongue flit over the tip and circled it, sending pleasant tingles spreading over her skin with each stroke. By the time he sucked it between his lips, he'd reduced her to a trembling mess against the sheets.

Then his thumb brushed against her core, and the first climax shuddered through her. At the pinnacle of her orgasm, his fingers slid free for the true lovemaking to begin. He joined their bodies in a single stroke, the power behind it prompting her to wrap both legs around his hips.

Every inch of him brought her to exquisite ecstasy. Her nails scored his upper back, and powerful muscle shifted, flexing beneath her fingers. They moved together as one in a choreographed dance of relentless thrusts and fleeting battles for dominance, knocking pillows to the floor as they rolled across the mattress.

"You like that?" he asked.

"Yes!"

"I'm going to taste you after this," he promised in a low voice, gruffer than usual. It ran shivers down her spine.

There was something primal about his take-charge attitude that made her feel dominated and cherished all at once.

"So close," she hissed between her teeth.

"Me too, *querida*."

Her body flushed hot with pleasure and sweat gleamed against his broad shoulders. One little word of Portuguese brought the end. Every muscle in her body pulled tight as liquid bliss coursed through her veins, sizzling down to the tips of every nerve. Above her, Zac squeezed his eyes shut and groaned in mutual ecstasy, back rigid during his release.

Robbed of every scrap of energy, even the strength to lift her head, she sank bonelessly against the rumpled sheets. Aftershocks rippled through her body in cresting waves as she dragged in thirsty lungfuls of air. In the moments afterward as she came down from the incredible high, she lost track of time. It could have been hours or even mere minutes, time becoming relative and inconsequential.

Zac's chuckle warmed her damp neck as he nuzzled her. River's curves cradled him just right, the bulk of his weight propped on both elbows. "We're not done yet," he murmured in a low voice. "I did promise to taste you, and I am a man of my word."

"More?" her voice creaked higher in pitch.

"More," he affirmed. He turned his head and kissed the hot pulse point below her ear. "Perhaps all night."

Goddess save me, River thought as his descent began. *How am I going to survive him?*

Or maybe she should have been thanking Hecate for him instead. She didn't need to be saved; she needed the stamina and endurance to match him.

CHAPTER 8

River awakened to find Zacarias snoozing beside her. They'd overslept, tangled in her rumpled sheets and wrapped in each other's arms. His peaceful features appeared almost boyish as he slumbered, relaxed and unlined by the worries of running a multi-million-dollar business. Tenderly, she kissed his brow and soaked in the radiant warmth he emitted.

I can't believe last night happened, she thought. It was the best sex of her life, the kind that made her lament all the time they'd spent not having sex out of some misguided need to prove they were hot for more than physical contact.

"Morning, beautiful," a drowsy voice spoke to her.

She leaned back and gazed into his half-lidded eyes. A hint of green peeked through Zac's thick lashes. "Morning, sleepyhead. About time you got up."

"Maybe I've been up for a while, waiting for you to wake up first," he countered.

"That didn't even make sense."

"Damn, you're right." He stretched out, reminding her of a languid cat awakening from a nap. He yawned again.

Then his eyes wandered from the sheets pooled at her waist, to her bare breasts.

Suddenly shy, she tugged the sheet up with one hand, only for Zac to take her by the wrist and draw her hand down to the mattress. With her grip of the sheets lost, they pooled around her waist and hips again.

"Don't," he murmured. "You're beautiful to look at. Every curve, every inch, all mine."

His hand traced down her side and over her hip, then skimmed across her thigh, leaving a heated trail across her skin. She yearned for more, and he gave freely. Soft touches became explorative caresses until their bodies twined together in bliss.

She'd never had a better wake-up call.

"What time is it?"

River twisted in bed to peek behind at the Halloween-themed clock on the wall. "Almost noon."

"Crap, I better get moving then."

Her bubble of elation popped, all hopes of coffee, breakfast, and a shared shower dashed in seconds. "Do you have to go?"

"As much as I'd like to hang with you for another round, I'm supposed to check in at the office today and lay down the law about our deadlines with Harrison. Think you can survive without me?" he asked before leaving the bed.

"I've survived without you a pretty long while," she replied dryly.

Zac grinned. "You never know. Dinner at my place?" he offered as a consolation.

"Only if you grill."

"On the condition that you make those awesome rolls again, it's a date."

They parted ways, and River hurried into the shower. Buzzing with too much energy to remain at home on the computer all day, she grabbed her car keys and headed out to a local cafe to read and sip coffee while surrounded by the fragrance of roasted coffee and vanilla bean.

Sassy had sent her an advanced reader copy of the upcoming shapeshifter novel, making her wonder sometimes if her author friend was part of their world and in the know.

Maybe he was. River pondered it. Differentiating typical shifters from humans wasn't as easy as recognizing other paranormal beings. She could spy a dragon a mile away from their eerie eyes and unusual body language. She recognized *most* other witches easily and had met a magician or two over the years, although they were rare and came along infrequently.

Ordinary shifters weren't so easy unless they made no effort to hide it like the dude with the plantation full of wild wolves. Everything about him screamed "werewolf alpha" from a mile away.

Behind her, an argument broke out in the cafe line. She sighed and stole a glance over her shoulder in time to see two teens facing off in front of the register. The town had been full of micro-aggressions and conflict for weeks, and still none of the local witches had answers. On the edge of her seat, she watched and waited. She twirled one of the bangles on her wrist and eyed them.

Was it safe to intervene with magic? She knew those two kids, one of them the town sheriff's son, the other the oldest kid of one of their local hospital's only six nurses. Louis and Sam were good pals on the Atropos basketball team, and they *never* fought.

The barista was a new face, a high school girl named Jenny according to her name tag. The school must have just let out for so many teens to swarm the cafe. "I'm sorry. I didn't see you were in line, so I—"

Sam cut her off. "Dude, I was in line first."

"Shove off, man. I was right here with my cookies, and you stepped in front of me," Louis said.

"Hey guys," Jenny said. "It'll just take a second."

Sam told the barista what she could put in her mouth. Her face mottled red and purple, and anger swept through River.

The kids continued to exchange words, growing more vulgar and rude by the second.

River jumped up from her seat and hurried over, banging her hip on the edge of the table in her haste to diffuse the situation. When she reached the counter, she noticed the café's owner en route from the stockroom. If Ginger interrupted the fight, she'd kick both teens out the door or call the police.

"Hey!" River called. She placed a hand on both boys' shoulders, imbuing some of her happy and warm, caffeine-enhanced thoughts into their testosterone-filled bodies— like teens weren't hormonal enough without negative magic affecting their temperaments. "Why don't you just chill and give her a chance to get your latte. Do you seriously want your dad to have to pick you up and take you to jail because you're being a hothead, Louis?"

Louis crinkled his bag of shortbread cookies and shook his head while avoiding eye contact. "No, ma'am."

"And do you want your mom to leave the hospital early to bail you out?" she asked Sam.

His face surged red. "No. She'll eat me alive."

"Is this worth it?"

They shook their heads.

The fight had ended before it came to blows, *and* before Ginger could lay down the law. With a little encouragement, River convinced both teens to depart through separate doors. River blew out a breath. The tension cinching her chest eased, but the overwhelming sense of despair didn't release her completely. Something had its talons hooked in her town, and she had no idea how to fix it.

Ginger stepped up to the counter and sighed. "Thanks, River. I really don't know what got into those two hotheads. They're never like that. They come in every day, but they don't cause trouble."

"Yeah, I don't know what got into them either."

Ginger placed a cup on the counter. "Here. You take Louis's latte, on the house."

River smiled in appreciation and slunk back to her table with the hot drink. Now she had two, and wryly thought she'd be awake until dawn. Accepting the inevitable, she enjoyed a long drink from her initial order, savoring the green-tinged drink's sweet vanilla and matcha tea flavor.

The moment she returned to her novel, a friendly voice filled with southern charm and kindness greeted her. "Hey, River, we haven't seen you for a while."

She twisted around and smiled up at a middle-aged woman behind her chair. Pam Wiggins, a school teacher who used to live across the street from River, smiled back at her. Her son Jack had gotten so big since she used to watch him while his mother tutored struggling English students after class. Back then, Jack would hop off the school bus near her house, and she'd feed him cookies and milk until his mother came home.

"Hey, guys! How's it going?"

"We stopped by to get a couple pumpkin cream cheese scones," Pam said. "Didn't expect the front row fight seats, though."

"Louis has always been a bully," Jack muttered. He took a bite of his scone and wiped crumbs from his mouth. "I guess that's what happens when your dad is the police chief. You can get away with doing whatever you want."

River's stomach rumbled. "That looks delicious."

"I bought two, Miss River. You can have one of mine," Jack offered.

"Thanks, Jack, but I probably…" One glance at the creamy delights through the glass at the counter changed her mind, and she relented. It'd be perfect to go with her free latte. "Sure. Thanks, hon."

He beamed up at her and offered the bag with his extra sweet, making her miss those afternoons together of watching cartoons and snacking together.

But I am sooooo not ready for kids, River reminded herself. At her age, most of her friends had one or two, but she didn't consider thirty-one to be the end of her biological clock either.

"Go sit down and read a while so Miss River and I can talk," Pam coaxed him.

"Sure, Mom." Jack headed over to the small reading nook the cafe owners had set up for kids. He flopped down on a beanbag and pulled a graphic novel out of his backpack with an illustration of a gun-wielding mutant girl on the cover.

"Mind if I join you?" Pam asked.

River gestured to the empty seat across from her. "Please. Wow, how long has it been since we talked?"

"A few months at least. By the time I get home, finish up chores, and make dinner, all I want to do is go to bed." Pam chuckled and gave her a rueful smile. "I'm a lazy friend."

"You're not the only one. I'm practically a recluse at the best of times. So catch me up, how are things?"

"The usual chaos when a new school year begins. I had detention duty last week. Five students, if you can believe it. Jack's doing good though. He complains about his tough teacher, but the structure is good for him."

"He's a good kid. Still gets frustrated though?"

"Yeah, but he's doing better. Your aromatherapy tips still work great. What about you?"

"Well…" Finished with her original drink, she picked up the caramel mocha latte the barista gifted her.

"Remember that hot Brazilian dude who moved in earlier this year?"

"Yeah, what about him?"

"We're kinda dating now. We have been for over a month."

Pam pushed her in the shoulder. "Get out of here."

"I swear it. He's so sweet."

"I'm glad you're finally dating again after that disaster with the hot firefighter dude."

Ugh. The ex she couldn't wait to toss out of her place. "Me too. He was an asshole."

"And judgmental about your Wiccan stuff."

"Yeah. I told him I'd date a Satanist next in his honor. I just know he told his mom about it first chance." Despite her bluff and all of her intentions of hitting up some online dating apps to check out the local Pagan social scene, she'd ended up dating a Catholic who never followed the rules. River grinned. "So, speaking of men, I ran into Joe a week or two ago at the grocer. He looked good. Talked about you two some, which made me wonder if you guys were getting back together."

Pam shrugged and lowered her voice. "I don't know. He came by last weekend, but… I know he'd been seeing someone over the summer and I don't want to rush back into anything, you know?"

"What's Jack think about it?"

"He loves his father. The divorce was rough on him."

"Yeah, I remember. Still, if things were heading that way, would you *want* to give him another chance?"

Pam's shy smile answered the question for her. "I guess I've thought of it sometimes… We split up because he wouldn't work or keep a job. He was always drunk and blowing through our money."

"And now he's always away working."

"He's been paying the mortgage and fixed the roof for us," Pam admitted. "We're going to have him over for dinner Friday to say thanks for what he's done, even if it was once his house too."

"Good. Maybe start slow and see how you feel about it then."

They spoke for a while longer before Jack bounced up off the beanbag and came over to buzz around his mother. He leaned against Pam's side and complained loudly, "Moooooom. I'm starving. I need more than sweets after school."

"That's my queue to go make meatloaf." Pam laughed at her son's horrified expression and stood. "It was good seeing you again, River."

"You too. Don't be a stranger."

***

The scent of grilled onions, burgers, and wolf reached Zacarias before his friend walked through the door with one of their mortal pals trailing behind him. They both carried a brown bag from the local Sonic Drive-In.

Zac's computer clock read a quarter after one, confirming along with his rumbling belly it was long past time to eat after sleeping in past lunch and hustling to work on an empty stomach. He looked up from the screen and gave them a grin.

"Sup, Tommy? Darrell? One of those is for me, right?"

Since Zac's decision to move to Atropos, Tommy and Harrison had become the two best friends he could ask for. They'd always been friendly to one another back when Zac was one of Harrison's employees, but working alongside him after the merger had only tightened their bond.

Tommy placed a bag on the desk then folded his beefy arms across his chest. All of his bulk made Zac look and feel like a child by comparison. "You know it, man. I heard you're sitting around here causing hell, so I figured it was time to feed the beast. We can't have you tearing this place apart because you're hangry."

After rummaging through the bag for his cheese sticks, Zac grunted and stuffed one in his mouth. "We're behind on a deadline. I'm not hangry," he replied around a mouthful of food. No one would believe him.

"Sucks. You're still gonna come to paintball though tomorrow, right?" Darrell asked.

"Yeah, no flaking out to work, or we'll have to drag you there the hard way," Tommy threatened. "Don't think I won't do it."

Of the three humans who made up their tight-knit group of friends, Darrell showed the most interest in the supernatural. An eager grin spread over his face. "Man, I'd sorta love to see a showdown between y'all. Wolf versus jaguar. It'd be pretty spectacular." He ran his fingers through his narrow dreads and pushed them back from his face.

Zac rolled his eyes. "Pretty sure I could take him."

Tommy scoffed. "Whatever, kitty cat."

"Sounds like a challenge," Harrison called in through the door. "Do we need to arrange some kind of royal rumble in your backyard? Think of how much money it'll make if we charge admission prices to the rest of the shifter community, dude."

"It'd have to be his, not mine," Zac reminded them between bites of his bacon cheeseburger. "I'm not sure how my girl would react to a pair of enormous wild animals brawling on her flower beds, and I don't want animal control called on me."

"Still haven't told her yet?" Darrell asked.

"No wonder he's been staring at the screen without doing any actual work despite barking orders at us." Harrison moved into the doorway and leaned against the frame. "That what you been distracted about?"

"Kinda, and I am doing work. For your information, bro, I was reading the beta feedback and looking at the coding behind that boss battle glitch. I think I can fix it."

Harrison chuckled. "If you say so."

"Hey," Darrell said. "Did you ever consider she might already know?"

"Nah, it'd be obvious if she knew, wouldn't it? I mean, I knew right off Harrison and Tommy were shifters because we can smell it on each other. She's not a shifter."

"Doesn't mean she wouldn't be in the know. Y'all are friends with plenty of humans who know," Darrell reminded him gently.

Tommy rubbed the back of his neck. "There's that. I've also seen her with the local witch a lot over the past couple years."

"The what?"

"The local witch. Atropos has its own magic user in town. You've probably seen her, especially if you've ever gone to the farmer's market. Older lady, lots of blonde hair, dresses sorta like a hippie. She sells soaps and herbal teas. Beauty creams and stuff."

Zac stared at him. "So does River. At what point were you going to tell me any of this?"

"Hey, I didn't think there was much to tell. I'm not a gossip." Tommy plopped down in a seat, leaned back, and kicked his feet up on the desk. Zac pushed them right back off.

"Anyway, now you do know."

"Still, that's not an easy subject to bring up. 'Hey, River, do you think supernatural beings are real?' She'll look at me like I'm nuts if you guys are wrong. Besides, I don't pick up the scent of magic around her or her place."

"They don't always shed a magical aura. Most magical types cover that up with spells to screw up shifter noses, while the weak ones smell like stardust and wizardry," Harrison said.

Zac shook his head and glanced at Darrell. "How'd the guys tell you?"

"Heh. Funny story, actually. I'd gone to see Tommy about something, hell if I recall now, and I caught him and Ceres mid shift. After staring at her naked—"

"For which she punched him," Tommy added cheerfully.

Darrell scowled and rubbed his chin. "Yeah, after Ceres punched me, it took a minute to process what I'd seen once my senses came back and I wasn't staring at the ceiling anymore. She hits like a Mack truck. I swear I spent three days wondering if someone flattened me in a hit and run."

"Then he spilled the beans to Bobby, so we said screw the secrecy thing and revealed the truth to Patrick at the same time," Harrison said.

"So, my advice is to take her aside one day when she's in a good mood, talk to her, and show her what you can do," Tommy said while taking a nonchalant lean on the chair's two rear legs. "Ceres has an uncle who showed his wife by stripping down and transforming. She took it well."

"I'm pretty sure, if I strip down, River's gonna have other ideas in her head."

"Yeah well, you can do that after she's realized she has her own super-sized kitty to snuggle or what the hell ever you want to do, dude. Just tell her. Most chicks are like Emma. They're indestructible and not fragile like you think. And if she does lose her shit or become a bitch like your shitty ex, then it wasn't meant to be."

Relief loosened the tight knot in his chest. "Thanks, guys. I appreciate the advice. Really."

"Now get out of here," Harrison ordered before spilling him out of the desk chair. His agility kicked in and he made it onto his feet instead of the floor. The raven sighed. "Damn. Almost got you that time. Anyway, I'll finish up your coding. You go woo a girl."

Despite having a few hours of his workday left, Zac bowed out of the office and hurried home. An intimate dinner for two would provide him every chance to confess the truth to her.

Chapter 9

River left not too long after Pam and Jack. Time had slipped away during their talk, and she had a dinner date to bake for. She made a quick stop at the market for groceries then headed home. When she reached her driveway and killed the engine, her mobile phone rang with a disappointing call from her father instead of Zac. The sight of his number alone soured her good mood.

It wasn't that she didn't have a good relationship with her dad, it was that she didn't have much of one at all. He preferred to spend his time doting on the children he'd fathered in his most recent marriage instead, and River had long since accepted she wasn't the little boy he'd always wanted.

"Ugh. Screw that. He can rain on someone else's parade with his bullshit." She thumbed the reject button.

She made it inside the door just in time to catch an incoming call from Marcy too. With her computer off, the video request came in through her cell phone.

Chuckling at the change to her popularity, she hit the accept button. "Hey."

"What's happening, chica? Too busy to drop in a word these days?"

"You know, ever since we made up and began talking again, you've been awfully needy," River commented, eyeing her. "Are you bored of the island life? Is your new husband beating you? What's going on?"

"Pfft. Bored on *this* island? Never." Marcy adjusted her screen to display the gorgeous beach scenery behind her then popped her face back into view. "I miss you is all. I'm glad we're talking again, and I hope you'll come out to see me."

River ran her fingers through her silky strands, relieved to have a temporary reprieve from her thick coils. "I want to make up for all the time we've missed hanging out too. I told you, I'll think about it."

"You always say that, but all right, fine. If you don't come here, maybe I'll come to you and see this little town you've moved to." Tranquil waves crashed against the shore in the background, and then a golden, whiskered face suddenly lunged into the screen and touched it with a pink nose.

"Marcy? What the hell is that?"

"Philomena, stop it. You're on my keyboard!"

"Marcy?"

"Sorry. One of Teo's jaguars got in the way. She's always curious about the sounds coming out of my laptop," she explained.

"You have pet jaguars?"

Marcy laughed. "No, not pets. More like adopted members of the family. Teo's raised them since they were cubs. His islands are wildlife sanctuaries."

"Your guy sounds incredible."

"So does yours. And now that he isn't lingering over your shoulder, you can tell me about him."

"What's there to tell?"

"Let's start with the important bits. How big is he?"

"Marcy!" Her voice raised in alarm and humor. "What makes you think I even know?"

"Because you're glowing like a woman who had *great* sex. Or hit the lottery. And since you aren't making plans to come see me, I'm going to assume the latter didn't happen."

River feigned an exasperated sigh and slouched back in her seat. "Well, I could tell you it's none of your business, but… it was the best sex ever, girl. I'm pretty sure he has a battery port somewhere because I'm not sure where he gets the energy."

"Usually I'd say I'm jealous, but Teo has the same stamina. Guess we both lucked out, huh?"

They chatted while River mixed the ingredients for rolls in the kitchen. By the time she pulled them from the oven, Marcy had convinced her to give serious thought about visiting.

"Look, I gotta go, Zac's making me dinner. I'll talk to you tomorrow about the trip."

"So you'll come?"

"Yes, you nagging harpy. Talk to you later."

After concluding her video call, River piled the sweet rolls into a basket and layered a napkin over them. Barefoot, she crossed their shared front yard, cool grass beneath her toes before she reached his stoop.

Zac pulled open the door right before her knuckles struck against the wood. The idea that he'd been watching for her brought a humored grin to her face and a glowing pulse of pleasure. They sat on the couch with a rented movie and the best grilled salmon she'd ever put to her lips. The citrus and herb infused fish melted in her mouth like butter.

"So…" he began. "You gonna help me set up Halloween decorations tomorrow? There are only two weeks left, and I need to get on the ball. I could use your help."

"Halloween stuff? Ugh, well, I don't normally…"

"I had this awesome idea after watching a movie the other day, and I bought about a dozen skeletons I'm going to nail to the side of the house. I can do yours too if you want."

"I don't—"

"And I started working on a mannequin to sit in a chair on the porch beside the candy cauldron."

His eyes lit with excitement, silencing her. How the hell could she rain on his parade now by bitching about the silliness and inaccurate representation of witches? She sighed. The man was determined to have the scariest house in the neighborhood, and while she didn't normally care about the commercialized holiday, his enthusiasm became infectious. His smiles encouraged her, and by the end, she was laughing while he described his plans.

"All right, all right. You've won me over. I'll help you."

"You're the best." He punctuated his praise with a kiss.

"Uh-huh. You say that now. Anyway, I better get back to my place. I have to finish up a project."

"Crap, I guess the time did sneak up on us." He glanced at the clock. "There was something I wanted to talk to you about, but it can wait until tomorrow."

"You sure?"

"Yeah."

Forcing herself to separate from him after the next kiss, River wandered to the door with him in her shadow. He walked her as far as the stoop and then lingered on the porch while she let herself in next door.

A dark foyer greeted her, the lights off and computer monitor in the next room set to sleep. A tiny nightlight emitted a pale blue-green glow over the entrance hall where she removed her flip-flops by the door.

"Maybe I should get a cat." It would have been nice to return to a friendly creature. "Or a dog," she mumbled, reconsidering. Every cat River had ever known decided on its own terms when to be affectionate, but she'd yet to meet a dog that didn't fall over the moon for its owner.

Or one who didn't make a mess when left alone in a house.

"Yeah, no pets," she decided.

With a belly stuffed full of fish and iced tea, she popped into the kitchen and filled a glass of water to sip through the night. The cordless phone, set upright in the charging cradle beside her electric tea kettle, blinked continuously to alert her of missed calls. She sighed and plucked it up.

Her voicemail reported three missed calls from Dad. One missed call from Cynthia Jackson.

River listened to three voice messages laden with increasing levels of passive aggression, her father's usual tactic when he didn't get his way. She sighed and pressed the button to return the call to her mother.

"River? Hi, sweetie. Is everything okay?" she asked.

"Hi, Mommy. Everything is fine here." To avoid owning up to screening her father's calls, she followed it with an innocent, "Why do you ask?"

Mom hesitated. "You didn't answer your father's calls."

Ugh. I knew it. "I was out on a date and forgot my cell phone over at my place."

"You know how your father worries," her mother said, ever the peacemaker between her ex and child. River's parents had divorced shortly after she left for college, like they'd waited for her to be clear of the house to call it quits.

"Yeah, loves to worry everyone around him too with his crap," she grumbled.

"Well, it's how he shows he cares."

River grunted. "It's how he chases people away." She managed to say it without heat, accustomed to her mother's pacifism.

"Can you try to let it go, just this once?"

"I can forgive and forget, but he'll do it again. He always does it again. Dad's not happy unless he's running someone's life for them. Isn't that why you divorced?" River asked, gentling her voice to a soft tone.

"Okay, sweetie. How was your date?"

"It was nice. He grilled dinner for us and we watched a movie." Cradling the phone between her ear and shoulder, she wandered into the laundry room and unsnapped her jeans then kicked them into the pile.

"Now what's his name again?"

"Zacarias. His family is from Brazil, but he was born here."

"That's nice. Isn't he the neighbor you mentioned?"

River laughed. "You have a good memory."

"Of course I do. I'm glad you live near a man who can help you in case something happens, sweetheart."

"Mom, I can take care of myself. I have the same gift as you, remember?"

"I know, but sometimes…" She sighed, and then the underlying distress in her voice intensified. "I worry about you a little."

"Ugh, Mom. Stop. I can take care of myself. I have the gun Daddy gave me, and failing that, enough magic to blast a bear out of his cave. I'm fine."

"Okay. I love you. Call your dad and let him know you're all right."

"I will. Love you."

River ended the call. As she returned the phone to the cradle, something warm and humid skimmed over the back of her neck, tousling the loose strands hanging from her heavy bun. She whirled around on the spot to find nothing there.

Just her imagination. Her mother had put the fear of the unknown into her with speculations and motherly concern. She shook off the strange feeling and speed-dialed her father. He picked up on the second ring.

"Finally acknowledging me?"

"I was out today and didn't have my phone handy." It took every ounce of willpower she had not to snap the words at him. "Is everything okay?"

"Can't I check in on my daughter? You never call."

Because all you ever do is bitch about my lack of a real career. The bitter thought remained unvoiced. "Well, I'm calling now."

"How's my little girl doing?"

"Fine. Did you get the tickets I sent you for the gallery showing?"

"About that..."

River sighed and prepared herself for yet another weak excuse. The same thing happened back during her school days too. If it didn't involve sports of some kind, he always created a reason to miss any of his older child's accomplishments. Art, the science fair... hell, he even skipped her high school graduation. Her art scholarship hadn't been impressive enough for him to make the time in his busy schedule.

And now a prestigious gallery in San Antonio was going to show a selection of her digital art on printed canvas, and her dad wouldn't be there as usual.

"Don't worry about it." Shrugging off her disappointment became easier each time. She sipped water and went upstairs to her bedroom.

"I have a previous engagement that night."

"Okay," she replied.

"Don't be upset."

"I'm not upset," she said honestly. She'd had thirty-one years to lose faith in the man who conceived her.

A dark shape fluttered past the corner of her eye. She glanced toward it and saw nothing.

"I thought about driving down to see you this week."

Which he'll also cancel, she thought. "Sure, that sounds fine, Dad."

Something rustled behind her, like something sharp dragging over wood. River jerked around and faced the double sliding doors of the walk-in closet. One was partially open, two inches of black space between it and the frame.

She hadn't left the closet door open.

"River?"

Another scratching noise from inside the closet tore her concerns away from the upcoming exhibit.

"I'm still here, Dad. I... I think someone's in my place," she whispered, as if the intruder couldn't hear her.

"Get the Mossberg and light that motherfucka up, baby."

"Can't." The shotgun was in the closet on the shelf, with her Beretta beside it, placed there a week ago when she babysat a neighbor's toddler.

River held one hand out in front of her and concentrated. Scarlet light washed over her fist, emitted from the delicate ruby in her ring as she channeled the enchantments power. Prepared, she took another step forward.

The closet doors burst open and a flood of brown scorpions rushed across the floor. Through the cloud of wriggling bodies, amidst her clothing, she saw the vague shape of a person, and unfurling wings snapping open in the walk-in space. River shrieked and threw the phone before spinning on heel and bolting out the bedroom door.

As she stumbled into the hallway, tripping over her own feet, she fell into the wall and bruised her right elbow. Sharp pain radiated up and down her arm. When she reached the top of the stairs, she gazed down into the soulless, burning red eyes of a ghoul awaiting her at the bottom of the stairs in front of her coat closet. The skull's mouth opened, and it belched a cloud of locusts toward her. Shrieking and waving both hands around her face, she lost balance on the stairs, and despite fumbling for the rail, tipped over and rolled toward the bottom.

The edge of the stairs struck her hip. Her thigh. Her shoulder. River endured the longest two breaths of her life, every second flashing before her eyes.

Please, Goddess!

Somehow, she managed to get ahold of her cat's eye pendant as she struck the third step, and in the next heartbeat, she was in her feline shape. She recovered in midair and bounded up onto the stairway railing. The ghoul had been floating toward her, an ominous shade summoned from the beyond. Her heart raced inside her chest, and yowling loudly, she leapt down to the lower floor and bolted to the entrance. Seconds later, she slammed into the door in her human body, fumbled the lock, and tore the door open to stumble outside.

Clothed in only a T-shirt and panties, she raced onto the lawn sobbing. "Zac!" His porch light clicked on within moments.

"River?" he called out. He burst onto the porch with only a towel wrapped around his waist. The man's bright eyes filled with worry at the sight of her. Then he jogged over and took her in his arms. "What's wrong? What happened?"

She hurt everywhere from the fall, but the adrenaline pumping in her veins had no doubt dulled it. The pain would be worse in the morning. She jerked when his fingers skimmed her throbbing right arm and tried to kick start her brain into creating an excuse.

"River? *Querida*, you're scaring me. What happened?"

Her entire body shook, and it had nothing to do with the autumn breeze against her bare legs. "Something was in my house. I thought I saw something in my house."

"Something? Did a possum get in? You know what, never mind, I'll go have a look."

Panic swelled in her chest. "No, don't!" She shook her head and clutched his shirt with both hands.

"Is someone in your place? Are you hurt?" he demanded, holding onto her shoulders.

"A spider."

His brows shot up. "Bullshit. I've seen you lift spiders out of the garden before and move them aside. What happened in there? Did *someone* try to hurt you?" His jaw clenched and his handsome features hardened, fury transforming his face into something more terrifying than the ghoulish tormentor haunting her home.

"I… I think someone's inside," she fibbed, barely able to get the sobs to subside.

"Go inside my place."

"Zac—"

"Get inside. Now."

He took on a stern tone he'd never used before with authority ringing in his voice. Gentle hands guided River by the shoulders toward his side of the duplex, and then he took off at a brisk stride for her front door.

"But you don't have a weapon!"

"Don't need one," he replied.

River waited just beyond the threshold of Zac's place, leaning out the door and wringing her hands together while waiting for news. A tense five minutes of silence passed. All the while, she kicked herself and wondered why she allowed him to go alone.

What if that thing was still there, lurking, waiting for her and impartial about whoever it made into a victim? She shuddered.

The police arrived seconds after Zac exited, just as she'd gathered the courage to run in after him. Two officers of the Atropos Police Department looked at her hip-skimming T-shirt and panties, and then they glanced at Zac's unclothed state. She tugged at the hem and cleared her throat. She knew both of the guys, familiar faces from their town's six-man police team.

"We received a call from a Mr. Ronny Jackson about an intruder in his daughter's home," Officer Clark said.

"That's me," she answered meekly. But they already knew that.

"Can you tell us what happened, River?" Clark asked.

"I was on the phone with my dad when I heard something. Noises from my bedroom closet."

Officer Duncan, a scrawny middle-aged man with a gun bigger than him, eyed Zac enviously when her boyfriend slipped an arm around her shoulders. "And what's your part in this, sir?"

"She's my girlfriend. I live next door on the other side of the duplex and came out when I heard her screaming. I looked inside and didn't see anyone, but her closet stinks and the bedroom window was open. I also found the coat closet open near the foot of the stairs, and it had the same smell."

Holy shit.

The cops searched her place and concluded it was empty. Whoever or whatever she'd heard must have escaped out the window.

Had she locked her doors? Did she habitually set the house alarm? They asked question after question, and she confessed to leaving the door unlocked while at Zac's house for dinner. While their neighborhood grew and changed on occasion, it remained as safe as ever. Nobody stole from anyone in Atropos.

"You'd be surprised, ma'am. Besides, it never hurts to actually use the protection you have in place. Lock your doors and use your alarm system. Could have been a homeless drifter trying to take cover from the storm that's coming tonight," Officer Duncan drawled in his thick southern accent.

"That would explain the smell," Zac said dryly.

River waited until the two vehicles peeled away before she turned and struck her boyfriend square in the chest. "What were you going to fight him with, if there was a guy in there still?"

"Uh, with my fists," he answered like *she* was the crazy one.

"Naked?"

"It's not like he would have noticed while passed out on the floor," Zac pointed out. "Anyway, you wanna stay over with me tonight?"

After considering the options and whether she'd be safe overnight in her own home, River erred on the side of caution and clung to him with both hands. "Yes please, but can I use your phone to call my dad before he gets in his truck and drives five hours to check on me?"

"Sure."

Someone had meant more than giving her a scare. They had tried to kill her, and the house wouldn't be safe until it had undergone a thorough cleansing. But who?

River could only think of one person with a grudge that petty. This time she wasn't going to fight on her own. First thing in the morning when she got away from Zac, she would call in the circle.

***

It took most of the morning to convince Zacarias she was safe on her own and no longer hysterical. As soon as he left for work, she called Pythia and reported what happened without the risk of him overhearing their magical business. Less than an hour later, her mentor arrived with Daphne and Rhona in tow.

"What a fright you must have had." Daphne took River's hands in hers and squeezed her fingers.

"Don't fuss over the girl," Rhona chided. "We have work to do."

In a way, River appreciated the elder's matter-of-fact attitude. It helped to focus on the work and not the heart-stopping terror she'd experienced.

She welcomed the trio inside and led them to the closet by the stairs first. Pythia pressed her lips together and crinkled her nose while staring into the dimmed space. Upon extending a magic-detecting lantern closer to it, a single blue flame blazed and created ominous crackling noises before flaring up to consume the entire space inside the glass cube. Then it vanished, leaving only thin curls of smoke. "Someone used some dark mojo on you. I feel like we'll need more than cedar leaves and sage for this purification ritual."

Groaning in frustration and despair, River plopped onto the lowest step. "I had a guess. Do you see anything?"

Daphne crouched and reached inside the closet to rummage through River's shoes. After a few moments of searching, she withdrew a clay orb the size of a golf ball. Further investigation revealed a blend of herbs packed with dried locusts inside.

River flinched back from it when the foul thing fell apart in the other witch's hand. "Ew! Is that a—"

"Hex ball," Pythia finished for her. "A strong one too. Don't worry though, River, we'll get it all fixed up."

They moved upstairs to the bedroom and found a second hex ball tucked in the pocket of a sweater dress. River wanted to set the entire thing on fire. Maybe the whole house too, but something told her Zac wouldn't be pleased to find his share of their duplex aflame.

"This one is probably filled with scorpion husks. Unfortunately, your closet smells like a crypt now," Rhona grumbled.

"So do all of my clothes." The hex ball had left a fetid odor, moldy like an ancient sarcophagus had been opened in her home.

"It's unusual for any witch to hate someone enough to summon *two* night terrors. Do you think it was his ex-wife?" Daphne asked.

"Has to be," River answered while yanking down all her clothes from the hangers and tossing them into a laundry basket. She propped the shotgun against the wall and set the pistol on the bed. "She must have snuck in while I was at Zac's."

Pythia frowned. "The good news is that they're only active at night. The bad news is that you can't be in here alone past twilight until this entire house is cleansed in case either spirit has attached to your residence."

"Agreed," Rhona said. "We don't know what else she's left here for you. If we start now, we may finish before sunset."

After crumbling the hexes, the group of witches covered every square inch of the home, peeking beneath tables, looking beneath the bed, checking drawers, and hunting through the crawl space. They searched outside in the lawn and garden to little effect, finding nothing suspicious among the dry grass.

With both apparent threats eliminated, they performed the first cleansing with cedar leaves and sweet grass bound by yarn woven from the hair of a unicorn's tail. They prayed to the Goddess and offered the smoke to the four directions, beseeching her to bless the duplex and dissipate any malignancy left behind. A sweet fragrance filled the downstairs corridor, but River's heart sank with terror when they returned to the upper level where the worst of the negative energy remained. It lingered like a dark shroud upon her bedroom.

This is my home. This is my home. Lucia has no power here, she repeated over and over.

They cleared the upper floor and set out sandalwood incense in each room for an extra boost. Daphne opened all the eastward facing windows to let in the sun's rejuvenating energy. By the time they finished, the heaviness had lifted.

"That should be a good start. Ladies, let's get to cleaning now."

"Oh, Pythia, you don't have to do that," River protested.

"Nonsense. We need to make sure no trace of taint remains, and you get a *very* early spring cleaning."

Pythia blended a mixture from her array of essential oils into a bucket of hot water. Together, all four witches wiped every surface in the house. They paid extra attention to the closets until the rank smell became only a sour memory.

"Maybe runes of protection here?" Daphne asked, regarding the sliding glass doors leading from the kitchen to the backyard.

Rhona pursed her lips. "Yes, that should do perfectly."

"Do you think we have time for the front door as well, and the windows?" River asked.

"We should, yes. Then I'll stay with you tonight if it feels like anything has lingered."

Pythia was a good friend, and River hugged her tight, struck with a rush of gratitude. "What would I do without you?"

"Buy a new house," she teased. "But before we finish setting the wards, we need to get the rest of the shadow off of you."

"Me?"

"Yes, you."

Pythia spread a mat over the floor and urged River to lay down. Then she removed a single eagle feather from her bag.

"Is that one of Ian's?"

"Yes. I've never met a shifter so free with his feathers as Ian, but he's a natural at it. Rituals involving his feathers never fail."

Rhona dabbed precious oils on her chakra points while Daphne arranged crystals in a circle around the young witch's body. Each sweep of the eagle feather diminished the anguish and River's deep-rooted misery until she entered a meditative state where tranquility overruled all worries, fears, and dread.

Until then, she'd felt dirty. Tainted. Someone had defiled her home and sanctum, the one place she could feel safe. It was among one of the worst crimes one witch could commit against another.

Her attacker's hold over her popped like a soap bubble, gone as if nothing had occurred at all. River breathed the fresh air.

"One last thing." Pythia's impish grin and sparkling eyes hinted at mischief. She skipped away out the front door and returned a few moments later with two large pumpkins in her arms. Both Rhona and Daphne chortled at River's bewildered expression.

"Um… are we making pie?"

"Of course not, these aren't the right sort for baking. We're going to carve some jack-o'-lanterns to keep your spooks at bay."

"We'll leave you two to it," Daphne said. "Call us if you need anything."

"Thank you both for coming out," River said, while blinking away the tears beneath her lashes. "It means so much."

Rhona's motherly embrace brightened her spirits even more. "Never hesitate to call, dear. We're all sisters. And don't you worry, whoever did this will be punished to the full extent of our law."

Daphne snorted. "I believe I'll pay a visit to Miss Aguilera right now. If I find so much as a single scorpion tail…"

Once the two witches left together, Pythia and River set up their workstation on the kitchen table. They had barely finished hollowing them out when Zac's characteristic knock thumped against the door.

"That's probably Zac," River said as she hopped up. "We had planned to decorate the yards today." She leaned out the kitchen doorway and yelled for him to come in.

"River? I thought you'd still be over at my—whoa. What happened in here?"

"Cleaning," she told him, aiming her cheek up for a kiss when he stepped into the kitchen.

He sniffed the air and nodded in approval. "Feel free to spread some of the generosity over to my place if the cleaning bug bites you while I'm gone." His gaze darted to Pythia. "Oh, sorry, you have a guest."

"Zac, meet my friend Pythia. She and her friends helped me clean the place up."

"Pleasure to meet you, Pythia."

"You as well, Zac." She smiled. "River's said nothing but good things."

"Yeah? Well, hopefully she never goes back on that." He sniffed and glanced at both of them. "Did you light a fire in here? I smell smoke somewhere."

"Erm."

"I'll be in the garden," Pythia said in a breezy voice.

Before Zacarias, River had dated a douche who hadn't understood anything but mainstream religion. Her refusal to celebrate Christmas as he knew it had been the breaking point, their relationship strained enough when his mother asked some ignorant questions about her conducting animal sacrifices.

And then Curtis had accused her of sleeping with Zacarias, and she'd finally lost the last shred of patience. She imagined that once they broke up, his entire family breathed a sigh of relief and told him how lucky he was to have escaped being with a Satan worshipper.

"Pythia helped me cleanse the house," River said in a quiet voice.

Zacarias raised a brow. "I'm guessing you mean more than mopping."

"After, uh… the incident with the homeless dude, there was a negative vibe," she explained. "Pythia is my mentor. She helped me purify the house."

"Oh, yeah, that's right. You burn sage for clearing bad energy or something, right? Well, that's cool."

Well, that's cool?

"Ah. You were expecting me to be weirded out some, right?"

"A little, yeah."

Zacarias took it in casual stride like she'd told him they were having chicken for dinner. She giggled and threw both arms around his neck for a kiss he eagerly returned after cupping one of his hands against her ass.

"I guess that means I shouldn't count on you sleeping overnight at my place, huh?"

"I wouldn't count on it," she teased. "But if you ask nicely, your chances may improve."

CHAPTER 10

Harrison had the better office, won by a coin toss the day he and Zac took over the suite they'd leased after relocating the business from the tiny building in Atropos to San Antonio. Most of the time, they both lounged inside with their feet kicked up, drinking beers and looking over reports when there wasn't hard work to be done.

Their merger had brought together two independent game companies and created a heavyweight. They'd doubled their combined staff and increased their budgets exponentially.

Zacarias whistled at the numbers he'd printed out. "Hell yeah. The pre-order sales exceeded our predictions, man. This game's gonna be a hit."

"What about those digital art books?" Harrison asked. "You know we have thousands of orders for the collector's edition. Art's gotta be awesome."

"River said she'll work on them this weekend. She's fast and promised she can emulate the previous guy's style. Trust me. I didn't wanna hound her about it yesterday because someone broke into her place the night before."

Harrison sat up straight in his chair. "Someone broke into her place?"

Zac nodded. "Yeah, someone who smelled freaking awful hid in both of the closets. The cops thought it was a homeless person hoping to use her place to escape the storm. She was really shaken up by it though. She looked *petrified*."

"Can you blame her? Did you try to track it down?"

"Didn't have time. Cops got there, declared it was safe, and she stayed with me. She tossed and turned most of the night, and then the storm washed away any trail I might have had." Zac frowned. "They went out her bedroom window."

Harrison rubbed his chin thoughtfully. "From the *second* floor? Maybe we should send a wolf to scent it out."

I grunted. "My nose is as sensitive as Tommy's, thank you very much."

"Hey, I'm just saying. There's no harm in checking. So, what did she see? Did she ever see the guy?"

"No, that's the strange part about it. First, she claimed she saw a spider, and then she said some*one* might be in the house. She lied to me, man. River never lies. She's one of the most honest women I've ever met, next to Tommy's girl Emma."

"This gets weirder and weirder."

"It was like she was afraid to tell me what she really saw. Then get this, I come home yesterday and she's got a friend there, performing some kind of Wiccan cleansing ritual with sage bundles and everything. I think it may have been whoever Tommy mentioned. The hippie witch."

Harrison's brows shot up. "Now we're getting on to something."

"Yeah?"

"You know how some people assume all witches are the voodoo-and-sacrifice sort? Demon worshipping and calling on the devil and all that?"

"Yeah. But that's not true, right? It's just a dirty myth. At least, I don't get the whole Satanic ritual vibe off of River."

"Well... most witches aren't that sort. Every so often, the dark kind of witch pops up somewhere in an area, and wherever they go, they take their bad luck with them. That's why the Salem Witch Trials happened. History books may say it differently, but one bad witch got about a dozen good ones killed, along with a bunch of normal humans who had never touched a spell book."

The impromptu history lesson raised the hairs on the nape of Zac's neck, and he shivered despite the era lingering deep in their nation's past. Even if River practiced witchcraft, he'd kill before he let anyone harm her for it. "That's awful. How do you know all of this?"

"The supernatural community is pretty small. There's no excuse for not knowing our history, or who the resident shifters are in a given area."

Zac shot him the double birds. "Bite me. I can't be bothered to learn about paranormal history on top of what we need to know for the humans too."

"Plus, Dad's the leader of the raven shifters in our area, so I'm expected to know everyone and what they're up to at any given time. You never see him, but he's still aware of everything that's happening, who's with who, who's got grievances... My guess is she hasn't told you she can cast spells and sling hexes for the same reason you haven't told her you turn into a giant cat."

"Maybe I'll tell her tonight. Just get it over with and come clean. She's pretty understanding, so I can't imagine her freaking out about it."

"Good. Because it sounds like another witch tried to mess with your girl. If that's the case, I can ask Tommy to send a couple wolves from the pack to keep an eye on the house. Help her out and bust whoever's responsible."

"Thanks, man. Hey, if they do swing by to check things, can you tell them to be on the lookout for a black cat?"

"A black cat? You looking for a new girlfriend already?"

Zac punched him in the shoulder.

"Ow! That hurt, dude."

"Good."

"Fine. I'll tell them to look for your lost pet too."

"Thanks. I'm heading out, so shoot me a text when you talk to Tommy."

River stayed on his mind the entire drive home. It was time to come clean and let her know he was more than capable of helping against whatever or whoever had threatened her.

The light's in River's place were off when he pulled into the driveway. A quick knock on her door confirmed no one was home. Disappointment tightened his chest. Too restless to sit inside and wait, he decided to have a run instead. Too many days had passed since he let his inner beast free.

Besides, he had a cat to search for, and embarking on a hunt for her was the best distraction from the confession looming ahead. He missed his little *gatinha* and hoped to cross her path again.

Maybe prolonged disappearances weren't unusual for the black cat, but a surge of red-hot jealousy coursed through him when he imagined her safe and warm in some other man's lap.

His little black cat had shown enough courage during their most recent meeting that he wondered if she had some innate sense allowing her to see the human inside him. Or if when meeting him as a human, she'd known deep down he walked on four paws like her.

The thick woods to the rear of the duplex smelled like autumn: Fall leaves, moist earth, and the juniper which sprouted up at odd intervals among the sweetgum trees. He walked until clear of the backyard then stripped from his clothes and set them in a folded pile at the base of an oak tree.

Contrary to belief, shifting didn't hurt. There was a brief discomfort as bones, muscle, and skin shifted into new positions, but for the most part, it reminded him of the pleasant crack of popping his knuckles. The fleeting ache was swiftly forgotten as he bounded forward through the leaf-strewn growth.

Gatinha had a preference for the meadow, and as he hoped, he found her snoozing among the wildflowers. Her dark little body stood out against the vibrant greenery.

She was tiny in comparison to him, a fraction of his shifter bulk. Zac nudged her head with his whiskered muzzle, and she drowsily returned his greeting with a soft, motor purr.

I'll have her scanned for a microchip. If she isn't registered to someone, she belongs with me, he decided. If she had owners, well, they didn't deserve her.

Amused by the warm welcome, he tickled her round tummy with his nose until she squirmed and kicked with all four paws.

Did River like cats? He hoped so. She may have been a pagan, but he didn't want to stereotype her into the typical persona designated by movies and television. Worshipping nature and lighting candles didn't guarantee she'd want a furry feline around.

Tonight he would share his secret with her, but for now, he had a wriggly, adorable ball of fur to love. He swapped fur for flesh and knelt beside her on the cool grass. Gatinha, as he'd named her, stared initially, then jolted back when he reached toward her with one hand.

"It's still me. See? I'm no different now than I was before," he assured her. "Now you know my secret."

A beam of sunlight cast a warm glow against her dark fur, creating the illusion of a shimmer. Or so he thought. In the span of a heartbeat, his shy little Gatinha faded away, her petite figure replaced by his kneeling, wide-eyed girlfriend.

"River?"

"*Zac?*"

***

"It's *you?*" River stared at the naked man in front of her, for once too amazed by something else to appreciate the view.

"How the hell did you do that?" Zacarias demanded. "You don't smell like a shifter."

"Shifter? I'm not a shifter." She touched her necklace, running her thumb over the polished stone. "It's a magic spell."

"A spell," he repeated. "So you *are* a witch."

Neither one moved, mutual bewilderment leading them to stare at one another.

"And that makes you... a jaguar shifter. You're my jaguar."

"And you're my cat. You've been my cat all along." He groaned and rubbed his face in one hand, probably reminded of the many foolish and idiotic things he had uttered in the feline's presence.

River winced, shot through with guilt. "Zac—"

"Was it a joke to you?" He cut her off abruptly. "Coming to my house like this. Listening to me talk about my troubles?"

"No!"

"Then what the *fuck*, Riv? Why didn't you tell me?"

"You know damned well why I didn't tell you. Covens have a vow of secrecy, for the same reason your kind don't wander around the streets shifting in and out of human form. It's a secret!"

She couldn't do this. She couldn't argue with him now, not when all she wanted to do was confess she thought he was a gift from Goddess Hecate herself.

"You came into my house with me and behaved like a housecat. I sheltered you. You listened to me talk about my personal problems and never…" Zac drew in a deep breath and let his head tip back, eyes closed in thought. "I'm going home."

"Give me a moment to explain. Please," she whispered in a tiny voice. "It was never… I never wanted to deceive you. Not once. Most witches don't share this with their lovers until they're married, or close to marrying, and when I realized you didn't know Lucia was a witch, I—"

"Whoa! Wait, hold it. Back up a second." His eyes grew large. "Lucia is a witch?"

Oh crap. Cat's outta the bag now. "She tried to enchant you with a love spell. Several times. And I blocked her every time because you deserve better than that."

"The wine and drinks."

River nodded, the building tension in her throat preventing her from speaking. Tears burned her eyes and threatened to spill over her lashes. She'd never seen him so angry before.

"But not you?"

Her belly sank to her toes and the wind rushed from her lungs. The accusation left his features cold, lacking the warmth she'd come to love. Her entire body numbed, beginning with her fingers and toes then spreading throughout the rest of her body like she'd been encased in ice. "Zac…"

"But not you, right? How do I know you didn't do the same thing?"

"It's me, Zac! I would never… I protected you from her!"

"Suddenly, you went from being the casual neighbor next door to—" He stopped himself and dragged in a breath. Her heart jumped into her throat.

"Zac?" River whispered, hoping he would finish.

"I can't get you out of my mind," he finally admitted. "Whenever you're around, the jag inside of me wants to claim you. Wants to make you my bond mate. I've never felt this way about any woman in all of my life, even Luce. The whole time we were married, I never felt the urgency to claim her. My relatives told me the time would come. Eventually, my jag would wake up and realize she was mine… It never happened."

"But with me it did?" she asked, her voice tiny and hopeful. "I'd never use magic in that way because it's wrong. Because we get back what we put out."

"Yeah? Then what's my ex-wife getting back?" he spat out.

She paused to consider it. "I don't know, but her punishment for her wrongdoing isn't for me to decide. It'll come to her when it comes to her."

But if chance brought Lucia within choking distance of her, she'd mete out her punishment a little early.

"Or never," he said bitterly. "It was her, wasn't it? She broke into your home and did something."

"I don't have any concrete proof, but… yes, I'm pretty sure it was her," River whispered. She gazed up at him and waited at his mercy while shallow breaths whistled in and out of her lungs. Zac had never appeared so hard and cold before, his impassive features terrifying. "When did you plan to tell me you were a shifter?"

"I was waiting to see if I could trust you," he admitted. "Lucia tried to blackmail me about it, and we had to call in help from a dragon to straighten it out." Zac began to tell her the story, only for his voice to trail at the end as his eyes flared wide. "Holy shit. That's why he said it. Because she's a witch and part of this world. She hid it from me all this time."

They both stared at each other, mute from the revelation. She broke the silence first and stepped forward against him. The breath shuddered out of her chest when Zac's arms raised around her.

Thank you. "I'm sorry. I'm sorry for deceiving you. When you first picked me up that afternoon and took me into your house, I was petrified, but I didn't have a way to get out without revealing my ability to you. So I just waited until you opened the door and ran."

Zac said nothing.

She continued to babble. "And every time we'd cross paths, you were so friendly, so sad. It was the only time I could be with you and not feel like I'd put my foot in my mouth. Because you seemed lonely, like you needed it. It was never about deception for me. Never about wanting to use you."

His silence continued, but he didn't release her.

"Zac? Please speak to me," she whispered.

"I care about you a lot," he finally vocalized, his voice raw with emotion, thick as if he'd been holding it in. "I know why you did it, and you're right. I was lonely. All this time, it was you." He breathed out a deep sigh, filled with relief.

"I wanted to spend time with you without saying dumb things," she explained. "I saw a man who was good to me. But what I don't understand is how you didn't smell it was me. I thought all shifters had good noses."

In hindsight, Zac's comments about perfumes that wouldn't irritate his nose made sense.

"Your magic isn't innate like mine. It's a spell," he explained. "When I smell you now, you smell like my River. There's always a hint of sandalwood on your skin. And vanilla. Your kitty has the same scent, but it's like a mask she wears. It isn't *you*. I don't smell you beneath it all, and I don't smell the cat when you're... you." He inhaled slowly, breathing her in, making her tummy tighten and core clench.

"When I first saw you as a jaguar in the woods, I was afraid. I thought an illegal pet escaped from someone's property or was set free. Then you gave me kitty kisses." She giggled, relaxing in his arms, snuggling against the warmth, listening to the tranquil thump of his heartbeat. "And I was positive the Goddess sent you to me—that it was an omen because I'd done something good."

"Maybe she sent you to me instead." Zac's voice was a husky whisper.

River met him halfway when he dipped his head to kiss her. Both legs turned to jelly as his tongue probed the seal of her lips and urged them to part, and then she melted against him, eagerly curling her fingers against his muscular shoulders.

At last, when she couldn't take anymore without wanting to roll him beneath her in the autumn leaves, she leaned back and gazed into his half-lidded green eyes. "Let me see you again in your other shape."

He shifted at once, sprouting a midnight pelt over his bronzed skin and lowering to all fours. He was massive, a muscled feline body built for power and speed, a true hunter far from his native habitat. A rumbling noise came from his thick throat as she ran her fingers over the dark, soft fur.

She giggled as Zac's rough tongue slipped over her cheek.

He was as warm as a living heating pad. After cuddling with him in their human bodies, his jaguar form came as a complete contrast, so different from how it felt when they were fur against fur. She kissed the tip of his nose, and for a while they laid together in the grass for the sheer enjoyment of being together without the need for further conversation. Just his furry cheek to her throat and whiskers tickling her skin. They didn't budge until an hour later when her tummy rumbled and Zac shifted back to his human body to walk her back to the house.

"I can't believe you can do magic. That my ex can do it too. Shit, speaking of Lucia, what do we do about her? If I know my ex, she'll be around again. She's not going to give up because she lost once."

"Seven times," she corrected him.

"You're keeping track?"

"You bet I am. I was dismayed enough when I realized she was using love potions. They're not technically forbidden, but most covens frown on their use. I mean, it's the same thing as putting a roofie in someone's drink, or slipping them some Ecstasy. But what she did to my house? That's flat-out wrong."

"Now will you tell me what happened?"

The memory of the entity summoned to her home sent a chill racing down her spine. "It's called a night terror. It's a kind of evil spirit that comes out after sunset."

"I've heard stories of such things, but I always thought they were fables to scare children at night."

"Says the shifter." She unlocked the door and led the way inside.

"Ha, ha, ha. Point goes to you." Zacarias peered around the house after he kicked off his shoes. He sniffed the air, and now that she knew the reason wasn't her place smelling funky to him, it was the hottest thing in the world. "Say, is it safe in here now?"

"Yeah. Pythia knows her stuff. She and two other circle elders guided me through a full cleansing. We put up protections as well. Lucia may be able to hide her wrongdoing, but she won't be able to work her dark magic in my house again."

"Maybe I should have you all over to do my place."

"We did the entire perimeter, but you're on to a good idea, especially with Samhain approaching."

"Samhain?" he asked. Zac's puzzled look brought a chagrined smile to her features.

"Halloween."

"Oh yeah."

"It's one of our yearly Sabbats, meaning it's a time of power."

"When you fly around on your broomsticks?"

The friendly, affectionate tease earned him a smack to the shoulder. Sharing the truth with Zacarias had opened their relationship up to a whole new level since knowing he was also a member of the supernatural community meant she could talk to him about literally anything.

And now she had the help she'd need to foil anymore of Lucia's plans.

Bitch, you don't know what you're messing with, River thought. *I'm ready for you now.*

CHAPTER 11

Sharing the secret of his feline nature with River raised a monumental weight from Zac's shoulders. In the days following, they made jokes about his intentions and enjoyed strolls together through the woods in their four-legged forms without a shortage of laughter or amusement.

"I can't believe you were going to have me vaccinated and microchipped."

"And spayed." Zac grimaced. "I saw that tomcat chasing you one day."

"Ugh. I wish the neighbors would have *him* fixed. I have half a mind to kidnap him and pay to have it done myself. He's a menace."

"Maybe I need to step in next time he's sniffing around my female," he teased while walking his fingers over her bare back. Since their mutual coming out, they hadn't come up with many reasons to remain clothed around each other, preferring to spend the nights alone together instead of out in a crowd.

Best of all, they'd alternated between which side of the building to hang out, visiting his place one night and hers the next. Zac didn't know when it happened, but no matter where he laid down to rest at night, it felt like home.

Did she feel the same way? Looking down at the beauty beside him, snuggled into the sheets with her long curls wild and free against her shoulders, he had to wonder if there'd ever feel like a "right" time to become bonded.

Was there an appropriate time to wait?

"You ready to pass out candy tonight?" River asked. "I'm looking forward to seeing the kids freak out over your yard."

"Bought three big bags of chocolate."

River giggled. "You do realize you'll be left with most of it, right? Our corner of the neighborhood never gets as many trick-or-treaters because most of the neighbors are cheapskates. The older kids don't waste the time here, and the little ones stop coming around supper."

"More sweets for us, then. Speaking of which, I better get everything set up. Meet you outside around four?"

After dragging himself from her bed and into his clothes, he jogged back to his side of the duplex. Despite her predictions, Zac had a good feeling about the night. No one liked to miss a scary yard, and his was the best. He'd make their little corner the go-to place for all Halloweens to come, so badass all the teens would be texting each other to come check it out.

With the fog machine already in place, all that was left was to set up his wireless speakers and get dressed. He hit play on his haunted soundtrack then slipped into his colorful polyester suit. A ghoulish, custom-made mask with cherry red hair and yellowed teeth completed the look.

Then he armed himself with a plastic, blood-smeared pair of scissors.

When River turned to spot him behind her, a screech died in her throat, and she dumped her armload of lovingly filled candy bags on the floor.

"Haha!"

"Jerk," River grumbled. "Clowns give me the creeps."

He beamed.

While he made a few adjustments to the plastic skeletons scaling his side of the duplex, she placed glow sticks in the pumpkins, giving each one a different color to illuminate the frightening designs. A larger pair lit with candles remained on her front stoop.

Maybe she'd been a pessimist, or maybe the haunted yard lured people in, but a decent crowd began to wander through shortly after school let out. They came in packs, escorted by adults who wanted to photograph the both of them in the creepy graveyard they'd created.

"You're making fun of my clown suit, but was sexy witch the best you could do?" Zac joked.

"I'm sexy every day. This isn't a costume." She stuck out her tongue.

"Agreed."

In a brown leather corset over a fitted blouse, River looked more elegant than someone in the typical adult costume. Her jeans sported gold thread outlines of pentagrams on the rear pockets, and she'd tamed her curls into a buoyant mass of dark ringlets beneath a felted witch's hat with a curled tip.

Once night fell, Zac turned on the fog machine and strobe lights, not that they remained on for long. Their town had strict Halloween rules and a 9:00 p.m. curfew for all kids to abide by.

"You know, I remember trick-or-treating until almost midnight growing up." Zac stuffed a handful of Whoppers into his mouth before hefting the candy-filled cauldron up and carrying it to River's kitchen.

"Times, they are a-changing," she quipped back.

"Change sucks sometimes. So what are you doing for the rest of the night? Halloween marathon? Reading?"

He eased up behind her and tugged her up snug against his chest. Her startled squeak when his cold hands snuck between her blouse and skin brought a grin to his face.

"Um, well, I light a few candles for my loved ones who have passed away. Do you want to come out back with me?"

"I don't want to intrude on your ceremony, River," he replied.

She took his hand and squeezed it. "You wouldn't be. I want to share these things with you, as long as you're okay with it too."

"No, no," he assured her, "I'd like to join you."

"Good. Maybe after we can hit up the pile of movies you snuck over."

"I still can't believe you haven't seen any of the *Halloween* series. They're classics, *querida. Classics.*"

She rolled her eyes then led the way out to the backyard. A small flock of bats flew by overhead as River lit a small array of tea lights arranged on an outside altar.

Each candle accompanied a photograph. A picture of an old man in his eighties or nineties with thinning white hair and a big smile had been propped in the center.

"So how does this work?"

"I light an individual candle for any relatives or friends I've lost over the year, and one big candle to honor everyone from the past."

"Including pets." He pointed to a photograph of a gray-muzzled golden retriever.

"That's Jazz, my grandpa's dog. They both passed away right before you moved in. This way I can—"

A cold breeze snapped through the yard and extinguished the candles. At first he thought it was his imagination, but the shadows deepened, smothering the solar lamps decorating the yard. When Scuttling noises came from the bushes, Zac stepped between River and the source of the strange sounds, alert for anything out of the ordinary.

"I don't smell anything but old dirt. And..." A familiar, pungent odor assaulted his nose. The sheer intensity overwhelmed his senses, bringing tears to his eyes and dampening his sense of smell. He coughed into one hand as an itch crawled down his throat. "That is horrible. It's like death."

"It's her. She's trying again."

Scorpions flooded out from River's ornamental bushes in a living wave of chitinous bodies. She and Zac scrambled away from the edge of the patio, but the moment the stinging insects reached the cement, they went up in puffs of blue smoke as if they were never there to begin with.

"My wards are working!" River declared with triumph in her voice. "I know you're out there, Lucia. You can't fool me. Your night terror can't materialize here anymore!"

"So, the little witch has some tricks up her sleeve." Lucia stepped out from the shadows. "And you, Zac, prowling like a tomcat around a bitch in heat. Seeing you so desperate makes me want to puke."

"Bitches are for dogs, actually. Female cats are called queens," Zac offered, almost on reflex. "You know, the thing you've always aspired and failed to be."

Lucia sneered. "I could have given you everything, Zac. With your talent and my magic—"

"No, Lucia. You lied to me from day one of our marriage. There is no going back for us."

"Do you think you can be happy with *her*?"

He looked into River's tense features, then back to his ex-wife.

"Yes. Not only is she beautiful and intelligent, she's *honest*. She's never tried to control me with love potions," he gritted out. "And she hasn't cheated on me."

"Honey, that could hardly be called cheating. I was securing a career, making money for the both of us to support your company. Have you forgotten that without my support, you wouldn't have gotten as far as you did?"

He stared at her, a sense of incredulity warring against his rage. "Hopping on two other cocks secured your career?"

"She means she used magic, Zac. Sex magic to get some arrangement she wanted," River said. "Some witches pray to Lilith to get what they want. I'd guess she's one of them."

Lucia clapped her hands in slow, mock appreciation. Her husky chuckle raised the hairs on the nape of Zac's neck and sent revulsion spiraling through his gut.

"How'd you get away with it?" River asked. "I know the circle has dropped in on you more than once."

The other witch laughed. "Yes, thanks to your interference. But did you really think I would be so naive I'd contact Lilith in *my* home? That I would keep such damning evidence where your old biddies or anyone else could stumble over it?" She snorted in derision and flipped her hair while leveling a bejeweled finger at them. "No."

"Leave, Lucia. This is the last time I'm going to say it." Zac shifted his position each time Lucia moved, keeping himself between her and River.

"Then you leave me with no choice. If I can't have you, no one will. I would have preferred you to come willingly, but maybe an enthralled puppet will suit me better."

An invisible explosion struck his chest, striking hard with enough force to stop his heart. Like a leaf on the wind, he tumbled backward, skidding to a stop several yards behind River on the cement by the back door.

Everything hurt and fire raged in his pores. The air wouldn't return to his lungs; they'd seized from the pain. He'd bit his tongue when his teeth crashed together, filling his mouth with blood. Seconds passed before he gasped in the first hungry breath. He rolled onto his side in time to see River lunging between him and Lucia to backhand the next attack away like a tennis player spiking a serve. Her intervention granted him precious seconds to get off the ground, although it took all of his willpower to pick himself up. He didn't miss the blood dripping from her palm.

"Stay behind me, Zac!"

Watching the two of them go toe to toe reminded Zac of a video game battle of good versus evil, a brawl more epic than sitting front row for the saber battle between Count Dooku and Yoda.

He never thought he'd be able to tell anyone he had a girlfriend more awesome than a Jedi, but at that moment, he hoped to survive their encounter to brag on her to the guys.

Lucia's diamond rings, which he'd always thought were a sign of her vanity, glowed brighter than the stars before sizzling streaks of lightning leaped between her and them. When River threw up her arms, the golden bangles around her wrist sparkled in a thousand rainbow colors, releasing a bright wave of power that coalesced into a shimmering shield. The electric bolts crashed against it with a deafening roar, leaving white spots in his vision.

He blinked until his sight returned then stepped up behind River as the next blast shoved her back across the patio. He set his hands on her shoulder and hip, bracing her.

The ruby ring he'd yet to see River without glittered and sent up a plume of fire. It arced above her head then spiraled across twenty yards of open space into Lucia's defenses in a brilliant gold and scarlet flash explosion.

Dammit. The other witch barely winced. She didn't even blink from the exertion of fending River off. Another dark lance of energy carried past them to the house, where it drove into the brick exterior and blew several chunks into dust.

Shit!

A tree to the rear of Lucia became mulch as River deflected the next attack heading straight for them.

"She's so strong," River grunted. Sweat beaded her brow and dripped down her cheek. "She's tapping forces I'd never meddle with. Drawing power from the ground… and from… and from—" Pained, River cried out and staggered back.

He slid one arm around her waist and held her firmly in place. "You can do this."

"Zac, run. Get out of here and get help!"

"Hell no. I'm not leaving you here with her."

He'd die before abandoning her to face Lucia alone.

Debris from the nearest destroyed tree rose in the air under Lucia's command. The jagged splinters shot toward them like a lethal shotgun blast. River threw her hands up in a warding gesture, and the air before her wavered like distant heat waves. The smaller wood pieces burned into ash. The larger passed through and scraped against River's clothes and skin. A thin line of blood bloomed against her throat.

"On the count of three, let go of me and take cover behind the shed," she whispered.

"River—"

"Trust me. There are protections here."

He nodded.

"One. Two. Three." Putting his faith in River, Zac ducked aside as requested.

"Protections" was an understatement. River darted back toward the house and slapped her bloodied palm against the sliding glass door. Unfamiliar symbols flared vivid green against the glass and surrounding brick. The air crackled with a static charge, raising the hairs on his arms.

Lucia screamed in rage. She twisted a cuff on her wrist and hurled forth an energy bolt black as tar. It writhed and pulsed, a malignant presence given life, spearing through the air on a direct path toward River.

The curse splattered against River's shield like raindrops against a window, a beautiful and breathtaking black sheen wavering on the surface of the protective charm. For a moment, it resembled black opal, and then it recoiled and snapped back. Everything Lucia had sent hurdling toward River returned to her. It mowed through her defense and laid her out on the grass.

River sagged against the door, breathing heavy with an ashen tone to her face. Zac hurried to her side and stroked her cheek.

"River? River, are you all right?"

"Yeah. Just exhausted and in need of a breather." River offered a wan smile. "Is she down?"

"Yeah, you got her."

"Told you Pythia was good." Some of the color returned to her complexion.

"What are we going to do about her? I mean, telling the police she attacked us with magic will only get us locked up in the loony bin."

"We witches have our own justice system. She'll be tried and punished in accordance to that."

Lucia groaned from the grass. Half of her body appeared shriveled and weak, reminding him of when his great aunt declined after having a stroke. Despite her feeble appearance, Zac glowered at her without pity and suppressed the temptation to ask Harrison to contact his dragon associate again. He wondered if he was serious about eating her and if he'd appreciate the snack.

With one heaving breath, Lucia rolled to her side and glittered beneath the moonlight. After seeing River change a few times, he recognized the shimmer gathering around Lucia's body and dove forward from two legs onto four.

No. She's not gonna shift and escape this shit.

A smooth and effortless transition occurred, but everything appeared to be happening in slow motion. His ex-wife shrank and became smaller while a compact, winged outline glowed in the center of her willowy-thin shape.

I won't let her get away to torment River again. I'll snap her neck and kill her now before I allow it to happen.

"Master, help me!" the witch suddenly cried. "Please! I am your servant. I need your aid! Help me!" Attempting to ward him off with magic, Lucia raised both hands. Gale force whipped at his skin and reminded him of crawling through a hurricane. He powered through the cutting wind, her attack sharp as a thousand, invisible little blades whistling through his fur at once. Every nerve end sang with agony until his teeth closed around her wrist and he took her down to the ground.

"Zac!" River cried out.

Zac was half-tangled in his shirt, hindered by the cotton tee with his jeans around both rear paws, but none of that mattered because he had Lucia beneath him.

Then he lost her. The shrinking continued, and the lithe woman went from tanned skin to brown fur. Her beautiful face wrinkled and her clothing melted into her body, becoming one with her as he'd witnessed whenever River took her feline shape. Both of her slender arms elongated and distorted into wing-like appendages, which she beat and flapped quickly to escape.

A swipe from one paw batted her wing-arm against the patio. Her pained cry was a half-shriek, more animalistic than human. He'd broken it. Lucia ceased her struggles.

"She's down, Zac. You did it."

Zac returned to human form and knelt over the wounded bat, confused. His face and shoulders stung like a thousand papercuts had been salted then washed with rubbing alcohol. He touched both cheeks and exhaled in relief when his fingers came away dry. Just a spell.

"Well." River crouched down and watched Lucia flopping on the ground, helpless with a broken wing. The caramel brown fur covering her body was short and rough looking, her smushed face flatter than a bulldog's with an ugly, upturned nose.

"What the hell happened?"

"This," River said, as she held up an onyx bracelet, "is her focus charm. You ripped it away as she was changing form, and without this she can't become human again. It usually transforms with us so this can't happen, but your timing was impeccable, dude."

"So she's stuck like this?"

A big grin spread across her tired face. "Unless I give this back to her, she won't be able to tap into her human body. And she can't exactly make another one because…" River gestured toward the pathetic animal. "It's the risk that comes with taking up shapeshifting."

"Stuck as a bat. Ain't that a bitch."

"I'd say she definitely got back what she put into harassing you," River mused.

"So what do we do with her now?"

River fetched a sweatshirt from inside then tossed it over Lucia's helpless body. She scooped up the little bat and carried her into the house. Moments later, the dark-witch-turned-pest had a snug bed inside an unused shoebox, a squeaking, noisy thing with no power over either of them.

His girl smiled up at him, her crooked grin the most beautiful thing he'd ever seen. "You know, if it wouldn't put me on her level, I'd be tempted to find an animal rehab center."

The idea shocked Zac at first, and then as the seconds passed between them, he knew without a doubt he'd found the woman he wanted to spend the rest of his life standing beside. "Are you sure we can't?"

Epilogue

In the immediate aftermath of defeating Lucia, River called Pythia to inform the circle about their battle. Defeating Lucia had taken everything out of her, and she lacked the stamina to do anything more than slouch in a chair while Zacarias stood guard beside her.

A group of witches arrived within the hour to take the dark witch out of her possession, all carrying different scrying orbs, focus crystals, and tools of reading the energy surrounding the home.

They all came to the same conclusion, verifying River and Zac's account of what happened. A tremendous amount of dark energy had been used in her backyard and would require a thorough cleaning. By the time the circle ensured no lingering curses remained on the property, it had been nearly dawn. River passed out and didn't know what the hell happened afterward, only that she awakened in Zac's bed with his arms around her.

She didn't argue about his decision to baby her and thanked him profusely for serving her meals in bed. Sometime during the evening over steak and homemade shakes, she realized his sheets had become the perfect shelter—an inviting source of comfort more welcoming than her own bed.

The next day, they visited Pythia together at the older witch's behest. She urged them inside her home and settled them in the kitchen nook with biscuits and sweet tea. Zac eyed it and only drank when River encouraged him with a smile. She couldn't really blame him for being leery about drinking something offered by a stranger, especially a witch, after the treachery his ex-wife had dealt to him.

"Thanks to some help from the Atropos PD, we located and searched Lucia's car. She left it parked at the grocer and must have flown to your place," Pythia told them. "I'm ashamed to say I never thought to check it when we searched her home. It also didn't occur to me to question if she had a wild shape."

"Don't blame yourself," River said. "I didn't think of it either."

"I still can't believe you searched her place." Zac snickered and sipped his iced tea.

"Anyway, we found a rather curious talisman hanging from her mirror. Once Grace and I determined it was the source of the aggression in town, we destroyed it. The air already feels clearer."

Zac whistled. "So what, she slapped some bad mojo on Atropos?"

"No, it was more that she was sucking up the good energy, which left only the bad," Pythia said. "So much negativity left in the area caused the issues."

"For what purpose though?" River asked.

"I imagine it was to cover up her aura. You sensed she was up to no good, but her aura never showed any sign of such evil. And believe me River, looking at it now, you can see the blackness in her heart. She's spent a long time communicating with Lilith and other darker entities. It's written all over her soul."

As they discussed Lucia's wrongdoings, the amusement dimmed from Zac's eyes. He sighed and leaned back in his seat. "The last year or two of our marriage, I knew there was something off about her, but I never suspected magic."

River placed her hand on his knee and smiled up at him. "Not your fault."

"Still… I can't help but feel like something's still wrong," Zac said. "Did you hear what she said when your spell caught her at the end? It was weird… something. She called out for help."

Cocking her head to the side, Pythia studied them both. "Did she call Lilith for aid?"

"No, she wasn't praying," River clarified. "She actually used the word master."

"Hmm. That *is* concerning." Pythia drummed her fingers atop the table. "It sounds like she was calling on a coven master. Grudges enjoy using such archaic terms."

Her boyfriend perked up again. "Grudges?"

"A grudge is the collective noun for a group of dark witches," River explained to him. How the hell had he survived in their world so long without knowing the bare basics of paranormal society? Part of it endeared him to her, and sometimes she wanted to shake him for being so oblivious.

"Cool name. Mind if I steal that for a game?"

Both women laughed. "Sure. But then you also need to add in a spite of vampires," Pythia said. "Considering what just happened here, I don't think you have to worry about anyone coming after you."

Zac chuckled. "I guess I believe in your witchy karmic vengeance thing after all. Despite everything she did, it all worked out for us in the end. But isn't twenty years a long time?" A furrow creased his brow when he glanced at the hall leading to Pythia's office. Occasionally, one of Lucia's screeches and squeaks reached them.

"You're the last person I'd have expected to feel bad for her."

"It isn't that I feel bad, it just almost seems too much when she didn't actually hurt either of us. You kicked her ass, *querida*."

"And now two decades are going to kick her ass." Dealing with her boyfriend's crazy ex had robbed her of the sympathy to pity Lucia's plight. She couldn't imagine being sentenced to twenty years as a caged bat in Pythia's office, but there was no time like the present to teach her the hard lesson of being a warlock.

By the end of the week, life returned to normal for Zac and River. Thanks to enduring the entire traumatizing ordeal, she gave in to her friend's pleas and accepted a trip for two to the Yucatán. She and Zac had earned a vacation.

As far as his deadline and plans for the company, his buddy Harrison promised to pick up the slack for him. Once her boyfriend finished weaving a masterful tale of his sorceress girlfriend defeating his ex in magical combat, the guys he'd introduced her to stared at her in awe.

"Hey," Harrison asked. "Do you think you could do some motion capture spellcasting shit for us? Just sayin'."

She did that and more, finishing up the art she'd promised and spending a day in their studio before she and Zacarias flew away for the weekend. On her friend's tropical island paradise and under the protection of a dragon, she'd be free of all worries, including Pythia's concern that Lucia hadn't worked alone. Whoever her cohort had been, they'd slip up sooner or later.

As they cruised on the ferry toward the tropical island, River raised a hand to shield her eyes from the glorious sun overhead. Her friend Marcy bounced up and down on the pier, waving to them.

"I'm so ready for this vacation," River murmured. She squeezed Zac's hand and gazed at the approaching shoreline.

A year ago, if anyone had asked her, she would have never predicted so much happiness could exist, especially when the start of it had been born from Lucia's manipulation.

Out of darkness and into the light, River mused as they sailed into the next chapter of their lives together.

ABOUT THE AUTHOR

Vivienne Savage is a resident of a small town in rural Texas. While she isn't concocting sexy ways for shapeshifters and humans to find their match, she raises two children and works as a nurse in a rural retirement home.